Alphabet Animals

A to **Z** stories, parables and allegories for all ages

Hilary Arthur Amolins

For my son Zach

Your faith and love kept me strong.

Alphabet Animals

Table of contents (Themes)

74 **R**ebecca the raven. Sometimes it is good to change direction and do something completely different.

78 **S**oriana the swan. Sometimes you have to yell to be heard.

81 **T**ony the tarantula. Do whatever you do, but do it well and do it without hurting anybody else.

84 **U**kuru the ulysses butterfly. Don't rely on good looks alone. You need skills to prosper.

86 **V**ictor the vulture. Don't waste food. There are still too many people going hungry.

89 **W**aldo the walrus. Never stop learning.

95 **X**oxo the xenopus. Clean up after yourself. Don't leave a mess for others.

98 **Y**angtze the yak. Turn a disability into ability.

102 **Z**oe the zebu. When you cannot change your situation then learn how to make the most of it.

Adam the ant

Adam was getting bored. He wondered why nobody ever listened to him? He had good ideas.

"So what if I'm small! That doesn't mean I don't have big ideas!" he muttered. "I'm tired of being called a little runt!"

But like it or not, he was the little runt. When he was born, all the other brown ants marveled at his tiny size. There were about 100 other baby ants born the same day he was, and not one was smaller than Adam. They all grew very quickly but for some reason, Adam hardly grew at all. When they played outside the anthill, never too far mind you because they knew that trouble was a short hop away if they could not scurry back into the anthill, Adam was always one or two steps behind everybody else. I mean giant steps, not ant steps. Adam had heard stories about the giants but never seen one. It was told that the ground shook whenever they were near. And they used monster machines that chopped up anything in their path. The one good thing those monster machines did, is harvest the grass so that it was easy for the ants to carry food back to the anthill. But the noise of these monster machines so shook the earth, that some of the ant elders found they would lose parts of their shells from the rattling and pounding. They would also lose their hearing, but that did not seem to bother the ants as they grew old. They would then rely more on their touch, and ant legs were very sensitive. These risks were overlooked, because the fresh grass they were able to stockpile after the giants rolled their machines around, made the ants so full and healthy that they eventually worked their days around the risks presented by the monster machines.

One day, when Adam and his buddies were playing outside the anthill, a kind of tag game where you could only use your back legs to tag somebody, Adam decided he had had enough of lagging behind the group. He was going to go on a hike and show them all! He'd go on a long journey (50 feet in giant measure, a massive distance in ant measure) and come back with stories that would finally convince everybody he was not a runt.

"Then they will respect me and treat me like the other kids and not like a baby" he shouted out!

So off he went, heading for the big forest. When he had got about five giant feet away, he turned to look back at the anthill. He could barely make out its shape. Only the tip was visible, poking out from the tall grass like some volcanic sand hill.

"Oh boy, I wonder if I should be doing this? What if I get lost? Maybe I won't find my way back?"

These and many other questions swirled around inside his head; making him so dizzy he had to sit down.

"That's all I needed, just a few minutes to collect my thoughts" he said. "I can do this. I know I can do this!" And off he set again.

He was in very high grass just by the edge of the forest, a place teeming with new sounds and sights. Big, blue butterflies twirled around in the sky above. And when he turned around to see where the anthill was he could not make out its shape any more. But he knew more or less where it was, so Adam felt confident about sitting in this wondrous new place and enjoying the beauty all around him. Huge trees towered over him, and far, far above in the high branches he could make out the shapes of birds. He knew that those were very dangerous to ants, and whenever they were around, he had been taught that ants were to find immediate shelter. A thicket covered Adam so he was safe from these flying feathered creatures.

An old green cricket went bounding by and nodded his head at the little ant. "You're new to this area aren't you kid?" asked the old cricket. "I live just on the other side of that big pear tree" pointed Adam.

"Well you're quite the brave big ant venturing so far from home" replied the cricket.

Adam smiled and waved as he passed by, feeling so much like a big boy. There he was, all alone and far from home, nobody to yell at him or tell him how tiny he was. Wait until he told everybody a big old cricket had even greeted him and called him a big ant!

It felt so good to be there, that Adam became so relaxed he fell asleep. He dreamed of piles of fresh green grass and ripe pears bursting with flavour. Adam must have been sleeping for a solid twenty minutes, which is a very long time in ant time, when a loud and clanky metallic noise jolted him awake. His eyes popped wide open, and all four feet tensed at once. He was jumping right off the ground. The horrible rumbling sound was coming closer and closer. There was only one thing that made such a loud racket. The monster machine! It was coming from near the anthill! "Oh no!" screamed Adam! Adam backed into the forest; he knew that big trees and thickets also offered the best protection when the monster machine was around. The noise was now so deafening that he covered his ears with all four legs and closed his eyes.

"What am I closing my eyes for?" he shouted. "I am a big ant!" And so he forced his eyes open. What he saw made his whole body shake with fear. A huge giant was stomping by, a mere few feet in front of the thicket. And pulling the giant along, was a monster machine spitting out grass and sticks like a machine gun! The force of the wind hurricane like; it made the shrubs sway back and forth. Adam felt very lucky indeed, to be sitting a few feet inside the forest. The thick tangle of shrubs stopped the spinning and shooting sticks from getting to him. When the noise had died to a little rumble, Adam knew he just had to get home. What would he find?

Adam sprinted along the edge of the forest as fast as he could, heading for the anthill. And when he got within a few feet of his home, he froze in his tracks. "Oh no! This cannot be!" cried Adam. Where before, the anthill had reached high above the grass like a sandy mountain, there was now a crater carved flat across the top! Hundreds upon hundreds of ants were scurrying about in all directions. There was the dreaded panic in the air! The monster machine had run directly over top of the anthill chopping off everything above the ground! Ants were crying. Ants were dying. Worse still, the monster machine was coming back! So Adam ran. He ran and ran and ran! He did not stop running until he was totally out of breath and his legs could not move further. Adam collapsed to the ground and passed out totally exhausted.

"Hey kid, what are you doing lying here in the middle of the field?" shouted a big black ant. Adam opened his eyes with a start, and jumped to his feet. "Who are you?" he said. "Question is, who are you?" replied the black ant. "My name is Adam," responded Adam. "So Adam, what are you doing here by our anthill? And where is your family?" questioned the black ant. "They were killed when the big monster machine ran over our anthill" cried Adam.

But his voice only cracked a little as he spoke. He decided he was not going to show these black ants that he was scared. He had to be strong. There was nobody familiar to save him here, it was up to him. The black ant asked him which way his anthill was. When Adam looked around, he had no idea where he was. When he escaped from the monster machine, he had run so fast and for so long, that he was now at least 200 giant feet away from his old home. And even if he were to find it again, which was most unlikely, what was there left to find? By now the monster machine would have run over the anthill again, and anybody who had been alive when he returned from his expedition would have been scattered by the hurricane winds that blew from the machine. No, he was going to have to make it on his own.

"Well, listen kid. There's no room for strangers here. And besides, you're a brown ant. We're all black!" said the black ant. "I don't care if you're purple ants" replied Adam. "I just need a place to rest for a while. Then I'll be moving on". This seemed to satisfy the black ants, and they told him to follow them to their hill.

4

When they were about to enter the main hole, a few younger black ants ran over to see what the bigger adults were bringing back.

"Hey, who's the weird coloured guy?" asked the first young ant. "I'm not weird colour!" shouted back Adam "You're the weird colour."

That did not sit well with the young black ant, and he pushed Adam backwards. But the loss of his home and his solo journey had emboldened Adam. He pushed back, and he pushed hard. The young black ant went tumbling backwards and even knocked down one of his buddies as he fell over.

"Don't push me around!" yelled Adam. "I'm not a runt and you can't treat me like one." The adult black ant that had asked Adam all the questions looked at the young black and said with just a hint of reproach, "I think you better get used to this guy. He might be around here for a while." The black ant shrugged his shoulders as if to indicate that like it or not, they would find it difficult to rid themselves of this stubborn brown ant, at least in the short term. And with that, they all filed into the hole.

Adam spent the next few days resting and getting to know his new black friends, especially the one who had first pushed him. They became tight amigos and after about a week the young black approached Adam and said "Listen, Adam. I've asked my Dad and he says you can stay with us for as long as you want" "Do you want to? We'd like to have you with us."

What a change of heart that was! Adam thought about it for only a split second and realized he could be very comfy here. It surely would be better than wandering in the big forest all by himself. And so Adam stayed at the new anthill. Nobody ever pushed him around again or made mention of his different colour. He was just Adam, the new guy! Over time he even became a very respected elder in the new ant colony. Remember, the colour of your skin is irrelevant. Believe in yourself.

Billy beating bison

Billy was a 7-year-old Blackfoot Indian. He lived in a tepee on the great plains of the mid-west. It was a time when millions of buffalo roamed freely. The rhythms of Billy's tribe followed the buffalo as they arrived at the summer feeding grounds. Summer was a time of great rejoicing and feasting. The buffalo provided everything the Blackfoot required for their existence. The thick furs would keep Billy warm in winter and provide a soft cushion for sleeping. Even the bones found a use in various tools. And the wide shoulder clavicle ended up as a kind of hockey stick which the children used in their stick-ball game. It is said that our modern ice hockey game has its roots in the stick-ball game these Blackfoot boys and girls played on prairie grass. They used a round stone which was passed on from generation to generation. Stones were a rare commodity on the prairie, especially perfectly round ones, so the keeper of the stone was a very special person in the tribe. He was responsible for ensuring it was never lost or lent to anybody without the keeper also being present. As a result, the stone-keeper usually ended up being one of the best stick-ball players because of all the 'grass-time' he got.

Well, on this particular day, a breezy blue sky kind of day, with prairie grasses not yet so high that the ball disappeared under waves of gold and green, Billy was running around trying to keep up with the older boys in an early morning game of stick-ball. Smoke was drifting among the teepees as breakfast fires were urged into action. Billy's Mom shouted to him;

"Don't forget you have a meeting this morning with 'Sun in her hair'".

"Yeah, yeah momma" replied Billy.

'Sun in her hair' was the teacher of the younger boys, and she enjoyed meeting all her new students before classes started. Since the tribe would be living at this site for some weeks, hunting buffalo in their summer grazing grounds, it was a good time to organize lessons for the younger children.

"I won't forget momma" he shouted, and quickly disappeared over a ridge in hot pursuit of the ball. The whooping and hollering of the boys mimicked the shouting and singing of the men who would hunt buffalo in the coming weeks.

The ball had been struck very hard, and kept on rolling down the steep slope heading for the river. The older boys did not want to go after it, being just a tad lazy at this early hour. They also knew from experience the return trip up the ridge was quite exhausting. But Billy saw an opportunity to curry favour with the older boys so he volunteered to go after the ball.

"I'll go get it guys, I'll get the ball". And so he ran and jumped and tripped his way down the ridge. Unbeknownst to him, at the same time a small herd of about 50 bison were winding their way along the riverbank, munching on green tall grasses and blueberries that thrived along this stretch of river. Billy could not see them, nor could he hear the warning cries from the older boys waiting at the top of the ridge. They had a clearer sight line and saw the potential for disaster. Billy just barreled his way along the river bank to where he guessed the ball had stopped. As he lifted his head, he came eye to eye with the male bison leader of the pack!

They both stopped dead in their tracks, equally surprised to see each other. The stone ball was right at Billy's feet. The Bison snorted and pawed the ground, readying itself for a charge. All it saw was a danger to the herd. Billy snatched up the stone ball. Just as the bison hunched its shoulders, readying to demolish Billy where he stood, some kind of instinctive connection in his brain snapped Billy to action. He whipped the ball as hard as he could at the bison. Whether it was pure luck or intervention of Billy's guiding spirit (which of course had not yet been officially recognized since he was not yet of age to undergo the spirit ceremony) was a topic that would be debated for years amongst Billy's friends. Whatever it was, the stone ball struck the bison square on its nose causing blood to spurt out like a geyser. The bison cried out in pain, wheeled around and ran in the other direction, hooves churning in the mud, desperate to escape this assault on his nose. The rest of the herd did an about face and charged with the leader, back along the river bank and out of sight.

This entire scene was witnessed by the rest of the boys at the ridge top, their jaws dropping in unison, at first shaking their heads, not believing what they had just witnessed. There was no denying the thundering echo of the bison hooves as they rushed away from Billy, splashing up water and mud in their wake. The boys erupted into shouts of joy and young boy war whoops, attracting many of their kin to come and see what the commotion was all about. Billy retrieved the stone and made his way back up the ridge, his beaming smile threatening to split his face in half. The boys hoisted him onto their shoulders and danced their way back to the village, recounting the story to everybody who was rushing from the morning campfires to participate in this swelling crescendo of joy.

When 'Sun in her hair' and the medicine man got wind of this episode, they decided it must be a magical sign of good providence. Orders were given to prepare a morning feast with all the trimmings and special treats for the boys. There was no limit to the amount of aged bison jerky the boys indulged in. It was a rare occasion to partake of such a celebration before the first full moon was out, and everybody sang and danced the day and night away. The stone stick-ball that Billy had heaved at the Bison, was placed on the tip of the medicine man's ceremonial wooden staff. It was to become a sacred object under protection of the elders. But whenever Billy wanted to play stick-ball, he was the only one allowed to take this sacred stone for use in a game, such was the prestige he had acquired thru his daring act.

So of course, whenever a stick-ball game was planned, Billy was the first one asked to join, since all his buddies wanted to associate themselves with his heroic act. Billy was a hero, and from that day on, the new stone-keeper with the official name 'Billy beating bison.'

Confront difficult obstacles head on, don't back down from a challenge.

Cory the coyote

The banging and crashing could be heard by anyone and anything within 200 metres of Cory. He was running straight ahead thru the underbrush, keeping his head low so the hawthorns would not blind him. But his haunches and back were getting lacerated and chunks of his fur were trailing him like some kind of furry pathway markers. Hot on his heels was a pack of wolves upon whom Cory had stumbled while joy running through the forest. Joy running. That feeling you get when your feet, or in this case paws, seem to float above the ground. Once again, he had gotten himself into a pickle and was flying by the seat of his pants, desperate for a solution. No time to think of one, survival was the only objective at this point. How many times had his mother cautioned him about his reckless behaviour? Too many to count frankly. Yet here he was again, running between death and deliverance. Which side would he end up on?

Well, the wolves gave up the chase. Even they were not so angry as to race through a razor laced forest of hawthorns. They had made their point and knew Cory got the message. No more blind 'joy running' in this part of the forest.

Once he saw and accepted that the wolves had given up the chase, he slowed down to assess the damage. He was bleeding from numerous gashes. Nothing life threatening, but he was most certainly in need of medical attention. And so he made his way back to his mother's den.

"Oh my God!" exclaimed his mother, seeing him limping to the entrance of her well concealed lair. "Look at you! What on earth am I going to do with you?"

But now was not the time to answer this rhetorical question. She ushered the poor lad into the den and ministered to his wounds.

"You had best lay down and get some rest son. It's going to be a few days before you see daylight again. Those are nasty cuts. I don't even want to know how you got them. It will only make me angry with you."

And so Cory lay down on a soft bed of pine branches and was soon fast asleep. While he slept, his mother pondered the predicaments her son seemed to inevitably find himself in. It was like a kind of bizarre and pathological, relentless pursuit of death and destruction. She was at her wits end as to a solution. Muttering to herself and pacing the living room, she hardly ate anything over the coming days, worried as she was about her son's recovery. A couple days after Cory's stumbled return, mother coyote's answer presented itself at the front door.

"How ya doin' sister?" whispered a melodious voice.

"Oh Eddie, I'm so glad you are here." she responded. It was her older brother Eddie, he of numerous misadventures in his youth. "I just don't know what to do with Cory. One of these days his luck is going to run out and he won't make it back here to his home. Look at him. He's gouged with gashes, lucky the wolves gave up running after him. They at least have enough sense to not jeopardize their own health, even when in pursuit. What am I going to do Eddie?"

Eddie knew the answer. He had not just coincidentally wandered over to see his sister. Word of the wolves' chase had spread throughout the forest. It was hardly the first time Eddie had looked in on his sister and his nephew, to make sure they were safe. Ever since his brother had disappeared years ago, it was left to Eddie to protect the family. Not really a burden. He accepted his fate and took comfort and pride in the fact he was relied upon. Being single, it gave him purpose beyond mere self survival.

And so it was, that Cory left his mother's home a few days later, accompanied by his uncle Eddie. They trotted along in silence for the first couple hours. Eddie in the lead, Cory hot on his heels. Every now and then Eddie would slow to a walk, only to have Cory stumble into his backside and then mumble apologies.

"Cory. Keep your head up. I'm in the lead, so your only job is to keep your head up and your ears and eyes open. No daydreaming. You're not a tourist. There will be time aplenty for hanging around, but we have a journey ahead of us. And if we are to both get where we're going safely, I can't afford to worry about what you are doing or where you are. My job is to watch the way. Your job is to watch where you are going. Simple. OK?"

"OK uncle Eddie. It's just all so new and beautiful."

"Relax kid. We'll have lots of time to go touring later. For now just stay sharp."

And so they continued, with Cory only a couple more times now stumbling into his uncle. By nightfall they had arrived at uncle Eddie's lair. It was so well hidden that Cory at first questioned his uncle's memory.

"Are you sure uncle Eddie? I don't see any shelter here."

But Eddie knew exactly where he was. He padded along the river's edge to a slight dip in the bank, turned left into what seemed from a distance to be just a shadow, and disappeared from Cory's sight. Cory followed, and found himself inside a spacious lair, hidden behind a high sandbank that was anchored by several blueberry bushes.

"Wow uncle Eddie! This is cool!"

"Yes it actually is. The breeze comes off the river and keeps it nice and cool inside." he laughed. "But i know what you mean. It is pretty 'cool' too. It's well hidden. It's far from the usual places you'd find other coyotes which means it is far from the wolves too. "

And that segued into a discussion, well mostly presentation, about the importance of staying smart and keeping your wits about you when you were away from your pack. And if you chose to live solo, with no pack to rely on for backup, then it was doubly important to do that and to also plan well.

"Take tonight for example." said Eddie. "I'm hungry. I'm sure you are just as hungry. We could go out and find some critters, but it is dark outside and we have been on the road for hours. I'm exhausted. You must also be quite tired. So the smart plan would be what?"

Cory did not have to think long about that question. "We rest. Tomorrow is a new day with sunshine."

And with that, Eddie lay himself down, curled up and was soon asleep. Cory needed no encouragement. He joined his uncle in dreamland.

Over the coming days and weeks Eddie showed Cory several tricks and techniques of hunting and surviving on his own. One of the most important was to make a plan every morning before going out to hunt. Know how long a certain route is going to take and leave enough time to get back to your safe lair before nightfall. If your hunt is not going as well as you had hoped, then abandon it and make certain you are back home before night. Tomorrow brings another opportunity. You can survive a night on an empty stomach but it is not likely you will survive in a strange place with no shelter.

Keep your wits about you, plan well and you can live a long and fruitful life.

Diana the dolphin

Diana was getting tired of just following rules all the time. She was not a radical dolphin by any stretch. Diana was just a teenage dolphin who had only recently turned thirteen. It's not as if she had spent a whole lot of time on her own. Her mom and dad would leave her for a few hours at a time when they went fishing, but they would always return and Diana was with the pod for the times mom and dad were away. So in fact, she had never been alone. As she swam around in lazy circles she thought

"Why not? Why shouldn't I explore a little? What could go wrong?"

She was so bored with her routine. And being a teenager, she compared herself to the other teens in the pod. But they were all 15 and older. She was the youngest of the group.
"It's not fair that I can't go fishing on my own when all the others do."
But Diana failed to recognize that those two years made a big difference. Sure the other teens went away on their own, but never totally alone. There were always two or three who went fishing together. Diana was determined on this particular day. So when the adults were distracted by a huge gray whale, she zipped into overdrive and swam away from the pod.

"I'll always know where they are from all that sonar pinging and clicking. Sometimes that noise drives me crazy!"

Well, considering how strong dolphins are, it took but a mere minute before she was totally on her own, zipping thru the water. She pinged with delight, delighted in hearing her own pings, but then caught herself and said "I better be quiet or everybody will know I've gone." Diana swam further than she had ever gone before. In fact, she swam directly into the path of a pack of marauding sharks! They could not see

14

her, but her super dolphin sonar gave her the heads up before they clued in.

"Oh no, I have to hide, what am I going to do?" she said to herself. "If those sharks see me I'm for sure going to die. Oh me oh my!"

The sharks were getting closer and closer. If Diana did not act right away, she was a goner. "Oh my, what was I thinking going off on my own?" But this was no time to panic. She had to act. Diana dove down, deeper and deeper. She was losing light, but that was no matter to a dolphin. Her sonar told her that she was near a shelf. If she could make it to that, she could hide underneath it as the sharks passed overhead. She picked up her pace and did a sharp nose dive to the right. Diana ducked under a rock outcropping that was about 20 ft deep. "It should be enough" she nervously muttered. And then she waited. And waited. With the rock above her she could not determine if the sharks were there or not. She knew that if they had caught sound of her she would never see her pod again. And still she waited. Diana lay there as quietly as she could, not moving a muscle. Several minutes went by and still she waited. Diana knew that she better give the sharks as long as she could hold her breath. Her life depended on it. They were definitely the longest minutes of her life. Lucky for her, there were no other sea creatures to give away her position. Finally, she decided it must be OK. So she peeked out from the rock but only to look. She understood that to make any ping at this time would be a sure give away. No sign of the sharks!

"Oh thank you sea lord, for watching over me" she said, and then as slowly and quietly as she could (dolphins are very good at swimming without making any noise) she headed for the surface.

You would have thought that was enough excitement for one day. But no. Diana now felt empowered and wanted to see more of this forbidden world. Well, not really forbidden, just undiscovered. So she swam away in the opposite direction of the sharks. More amazing sights beheld her. She dipped her way through a massive bed of kelp, the red/green strands dipping and dancing like some orchestra of streamers.

A school of jelly fish were also bobbing and weaving up ahead. Diana knew to avoid those. She had learned in dolphin school that one bite from them and you could find yourself paralyzed.

As she was marveling at the sight, a strange kathump, kathump sound beat out from behind the jelly fish.

"Now that sounds a lot like those boats that we were told in school to avoid at all costs. But why on earth should we not be allowed to see new things?" she mused. So without giving it too much additional thought (Diana as you can see was being led by her desire to explore, and ignoring a lot of the rules she had learned) she gave the jelly fish a wide berth and headed for the sound. "Oh, it is so good to be free and on my own" she chirped in delight, having so soon forgotten the almost disastrous experience with the sharks.

Bang! She was stopped dead in her tracks. Could not move forward, could not move backward. "What is going on?" she said. Diana tried to do a power dive, but to no avail. She could not make any movement at all, aside from a little waggle of her tail fin. And the more she tried, the less she could move. Diana had swum right into the fishing trawler's net! She was caught tight. Locked in place by miles of mesh.

"Oh me, oh my!" she cried. But the more she thrashed and moved, the tighter the net grabbed at her. "Could this be my end? After beating those sharks could I be caught in this net forever?"

Well, not forever. As fate would have it, this entire process was being watched by a wise old sea turtle. This was a massive leather-back, probably about 400 years old. And it patiently watched as Diana continued her thrashing. It glided over to her, careful to avoid the net movement. This turtle had not got to be centuries old without having learned about sea dangers, trawler nets being at the top of its list of things to avoid. Diana noticed the turtle and gasped. "Help me Mr. Turtle, please help me." The turtle said nothing just floated along and watched. "Oh please Mr. Turtle, can you not help me?"

The turtle looked her right in the eyes and said "So how is it that you, a young dolphin if I may say so, has found yourself alone in such a predicament?" Diana responded. "Oh wise turtle, I decided to go see the world on my own. I was so tired of following rules, and now look at me."

"Well, first of all stop your thrashing about; it is only making things worse. The more you panic, the tighter the net gets" said Mr. Turtle. And so Diana stopped her thrashing about.

"There, now maybe we can take a closer look and see what we have here" said Mr. Turtle. He carefully moved to within a few meters of Diana and did a closer inspection. Diana started to wiggle again. The turtle moved back. "Now see here Missy, if you don't stop your panicking, you will be in a dearly awful mess." So Diana stopped and listened.

"Now" said the turtle "I can probably get you out of this mess, but you have to promise me something." "Anything" said Diana "Anything you say, I just want to get back to my pod".

"OK then" said Mr. Turtle. "Here is how we're going to do this. You have to promise me that you will not make any movement while I work. Because if you do you put us both in danger. Second, I will guide you back to your pod. I know where they are. And you young lady, will promise to never again, at least until you are much older, to go gallivanting about on your own. Is that a deal?"

"Oh yes, wise old turtle, I will gladly do this. I've seen quite enough of the sea world on my own today. It can be a dangerous place if one is not prepared."

So having come to that agreement, the turtle proceeded to carefully gnaw its way through the mesh. One by one, it released the nasty trawler net, chewing away and all the while being very careful to not get caught in any drift. This process took about 45 minutes to accomplish, and Diana was finally released. She chirped in joy, and swam happy circles around the turtle. "Thank you, thank you thank you, thank you!" And with that, she followed Mr. Turtle along. "Can't you swim any faster please? I do want to get back to my pod." The turtle looked at her and said, "Missy, remember our deal. You follow me and I will get you safely back." And so they wound their way thru the deep blue sea, arriving at her pod some 2 hours later where Dianna was greeted with chirps of joy from her pod, and where thanks were offered to the wise sea turtle.

Don't leave home before you are ready, never go somewhere without telling your mom and dad and listen to elders.

Edy the elephant

Edy was the smallest elephant in the herd. And also the quietest. Mom would always be trying to encourage her to speak up. But Edy was OK with just being in the background. She watched and learned. It had been like that since Edy was the smallest and youngest of Mom's babies. She had an extraordinarily large gathering, three baby elephants and all had survived the rigours of life in Africa. They were the largest land mammals, but another land mammal, at least some very ignorant ones, had decided that elephant tusks would make for pretty jewelery and other dust collecting ornaments. Things had improved recently with intervention of wonderful groups like the World Wildlife Fund and , International Ecotourism Society, but it was still a dangerous world for elephants.

Edy, at 7 years old (or young) had learned well enough, at least enough to stay alive. And sadly that was saying a lot. Survival was always something the herd understood. And that instinct passed almost genetically, by some kind of weird osmosis to each new generation. Edy understood she just had to survive. There was not a whole lot of laying in the hammock kind of time, if you know what I mean. One of the survival things the elephants always did, was their annual migration to find more food. That's the trouble with being an elephant. You just eat so much food!

During one migration across a river, Edy was late getting to the riverbank. Now being late in a migration has an entirely different context than being late for dinner, or being late for your bus. People will wait and there will be another bus. But a migration is another thing altogether. There is only one. It is timed to coincide with position of the moon, with generations of instinct, with impending change in food supply. Lots of things determine when the migration happens. Including the whim of the head bull. And if you're not there to join, you will be on your own. Protection of the herd is gone. You are just another single animal trying to survive. This time, Edy was late.

What had held her up was nothing significant. She had found herself down by the local stream just bathing and splashing around. She was having so much fun that she just plumb forgot that today was migration day! Silly really, when you consider that survival was the foremost thing in all elephants minds. Smelling the roses so to speak or just having fun were not things they commonly indulged in. But kids will be kids, no matter in what part of the world or what species you may be talking about. Edy, after all, was just a kid.

So you can picture her surprise when she came back to where the herd had been, after her afternoon of splashing and having fun, and found nobody! I mean absolutely nobody. Mom gone. Brothers gone. All her buddies gone. The entire herd had cleared out. She gave her head a shake.

"How could this happen? How could I not have heard?" she mused.

But considering kids can get into an entirely different dimension when playing, it was not a great surprise. Edy just got lost in her own world. And that world happened to be down the riverbank and out of earshot of the herd. Even her monster ears had failed her today. Well, that is not fair. They had not failed her, the sound of the moving herd was just up the riverbank but far enough away so that sound waves could not pick it up. Kind of like having a walkie-talkie in the mountains. If the signal cannot get past some immovable object, like a mountain, then there is no way the sound will travel to the next receiver. Edy, the receiver, was out of earshot. Standing at the top of the riverbank, she looked around. What had only a few hours ago been a massive collection of 13 elephants had now become a deserted and somewhat trampled savannah, occasionally dotted with a tree. There was still lots of vegetation around the riverbank, where the elephants would get their fill. But Edy could not possibly survive here on her own. She had to move.

Now, the migration route was pretty much set in advance. Except for a few years when rains came really late, the elephants had moved in the same north/south direction, crossing the river about 5 miles to the north. Edy figured that even including her private time in the river, she could maybe catch the herd in about 7 hours if she boogied. She dearly wanted to catch them before they crossed the river, because that was something no young elephant wanted to do on their own. Crocodiles had absolutely no fear of elephants, and if the crocodile was large enough and the elephant small enough, they would attack. Edy was small enough, and she knew it. So, off she went. She started at a kind of panic gallop but soon settled into a more comfortable trot. Edy realized there was no way she could go full out for 7 hours, so she had better conserve her energy. The route was not entirely unfamiliar to her. At seven years of age she had been doing this route for 7 years. Now, that was a far cry from the head bull's 64 years, but still it had given her a good sense of where to go.

She had been trotting along for about 4 hours when thunder clouds loomed in front. "Oh, Oh. This won't be good for crossing the river." she mused. And she was right. If a sudden tropical downpour were to happen, she would find herself in very deep doo doo if you know what I mean. So she picked up her pace a tad. The first droplets caught her in the ears. Not a lot, but she felt enough to know that rains were coming. Edy knew she had to conserve her energy and could not panic. So she quickened her pace a little, but not enough to jack up her heart rate too much. The rains were quite definitely rains now. Edy had to blink her eyes every few paces, to clear her vision. It was not raining that hard that she could not see, but it was evident from the darkening sky, that a serious downpour was in the works. The first one of the rainy season. The herd had enjoyed several months of sunshine, this a fact contrary to most biologists/zoologists who think animals love the rainy season. Are you kidding me? What's fun about hanging out in hours and hours of deluge, without any cover?

So on Edy trotted. She was getting close to the river crossing, but now the rain was pounding down. She had to slow her pace, because the ground was turning into a mucky mess. Edy figured she was about half an hour from the river crossing, but if she were to cross now, maybe it would give her a chance to get across without having to swim. Elephants, especially elephants on their own, did not like to lose foot contact with the ground. So she veered to the right and scampered down the river bank. What a surprise! The river was already 3 metres higher than usual, and it was teeming with crocodiles! She had committed herself now, because going back up the bank was out of the question. She had half slipped and slid down, so there was no way she could get back up. The crocs had noticed the unusual activity and started to mill about in the middle of the river. Edy knew what they were thinking. "Here I am, a lonely young elephant, on my own. I must look like dinner!" But to her credit she did not panic. Edy figured that the only way out of this mess was to work with the crocodiles and seem as if she was stronger than she really was.

"Hey, you, Mr. Crocodile!" she yelled. Well this took the crocodiles completely by surprise. They were more accustomed to young elephants panicking at the sight of twenty crocs! So they did not know what to make of Edy.

"Hey, you!" she yelled again, directing her conversation at the biggest croc in the bunch, figuring he would be the head honcho. Now, the big croc could not exactly ignore her, as the other crocs were watching him for his reaction. This was certainly something he had never encountered before. But he had to maintain some posture of dominance, at least for his groups, he answered: "And what would a young and tasty elephant be doing here on her own?"

The rest of the crocs bellowed in laughter, figuring this would make for a very delightful snack. "I'm here to cross the river and you guys are going to help me." said Edy. Well this caught the head croc totally by surprise. "Help you across the river?" was all he could answer.

"Yes" said Edy, " It is too deep for me to swim and my herd needs me, so you guys are going to help me." This was indeed a little too much for the croc brain to handle so he conferenced with his buddies. They snapped and jawed and snorted for a while, and head croc came back with this retort, "Why should we help you when it would be much easier to eat you?" Which of course brought another round of belly laughs from the others.

"Because my dad is head bull in our herd. And he is good friends with all the hippos here. So if he hears that his youngest daughter fell victim to some heinous crime by a bunch of ravenous crocs, well I hate to think what he would do."

Now that kind of a reply was totally out of the blue for the croc. He just stared at Edy without saying anything. But his buddies were jeering in the background. The head croc wheeled around and gave them an icy stare that shut everybody up tight. Like a crocodiles jaws snapping shut. He turned slowly to face Edy. "And how can we help you?" He asked. Edy, whose heart was racing a mile a minute, had to think super fast. "You and your buddies are going to make a floating bridge, and I am going to walk across to the other side." she replied.

Well this drew a chorus of whistles and boos and sundry other insults. But head croc shut them down. He knew, that if there was even a slight chance of this elephant being right in her boast, that his croc herd would indeed be in danger. He knew the memory of elephants, and understood that even if it took several years, the elephant herd would hunt him down if some harm were to come to this young lady. So he turned to face his herd and said "We're going to help this elephant cross the river."

They looked at him in disbelief and one of the bigger ones said "And what if we don't"? That remark was met by a quick snap of the head bulls jaws on the other crocs neck, enough to send him bellowing in pain to the back. "Anybody else have a problem with this plan?"

But nobody dared question him anymore. They proceeded to form a pontoon bridge, and Edy carefully stepped her way to the other side. When she got there, she turned to look at the head croc and said "This moment will not be forgotten. I will tell my father, and we will pass this story of friendship down through many generations. And should you ever find yourself in need of help, you know that our herd will be willing to help you and your kind. Good luck to you all." And with that, she scampered off and was quickly out of sight.

Within 2 hours Edy had met up with her herd and told them this story. They did not at first believe her, but the details and the miracle of her arriving at all, following such a rainy deluge, convinced them that Edy was telling truth. Her patience and quick thinking under stress had bought her a new life.

You don't have to be loud or aggressive but you need to be convincing.

Frankie the fish

Everybody has heard about the Loch Ness monster but not too many people know about the legend of Lake Consecon. This is a story about that legend. His name is Frankie.

Frankie's story starts several years ago. He was a tiny hatchling, eager to explore the shoreline and hunt for teeny tiny minnows. His mother had warned him about getting too close to shore but Frankie was more concerned (as is the case with most bass, they just love to eat) with finding snacks. And Bobby, a young lad who lived on the shores of the lake was walking the shore on that particular day, carrying his fishing net. He wasn't looking for Frankie in particular, but fate brought them together. Bobby saw Frankie before Frankie had time to react. And his net scooped into the shallows, snagging Frankie. Up came the net and there Frankie flipped and flopped, suspended in air.

"Awwright!" shouted Bobby. "I'm gonna take you home with me." And so he brought Frankie up from the shore and to his house. His mother saw him approach and asked what he had in the net. "It's a little bass Mom. Can I keep him? Can I? Can I?" His Mom thought for a second about making him put the fish back in the lake, but decided this would make for a good exercise in responsibility and besides, Bobby was so proud of his catch. "OK" said Mom. "But you have to promise that you will take care of it and feed it. And when it gets too big for that aquarium you'll have to bring it back to the lake. Promise?" "I promise" replied Bobby. "I promise Mom."

And he spent the rest of the day watching his fish swimming in the aquarium, bringing up stones from the lake and twigs and grass, creating a nice little surrounding for the fish.

Frankie at first was mortified about being in a glass house. He'd swim in circles, occasionally bumping his head into the glass, bruising his mouth and cheeks. It took several days until he got the hang of it. Bobby

25

would make sure the fish had insects and frogs and he even spent some time on his computer learning about habits of bass and what they liked to eat. His Mom was very proud of him and pleased that his computer time was not always dedicated to shooting up aliens or smashing cars into imaginary walls!

As time went by, months of time, Frankie grew larger and larger. His daily feedings had added several pounds and about a year later he was already 4 lbs. Now that is very big for a bass even in the wild. But for an aquarium bass it was huge! And several times in the past month, Frankie had jumped clear out of the aquarium, landing on the floor. Thankfully, Bobby or his Mom had been around to put him back in the tank, and they had to place a board over top of the tank. Mom knew the time had come to tell Bobby that the fish had to go back to the lake. She knew how attached he was to it and how difficult it would be for Bobby to give up the fish. But, they had agreed, and a promise is a promise.

"Ah no Mom, just a little longer! I'll get a bigger aquarium. I'll make sure he never jumps out again." pleaded Bobby.

"Bobby, you've taken very good care of your fish. That's not the problem. The problem is the fish has grown much too big and needs a wider world now. And we did make a promise a year ago, remember?"

Of course he did remember, but Bobby was desperate to keep the fish. "Mom, why can't I keep it? I'm taking good care of it." To which his mother again replied "Bobby, you are taking good care of it, but the fish needs a bigger home. It's not fair to the fish any longer. Bass need room to roam, and this is a big bass. He needs to get into a much bigger aquarium, and that aquarium is the lake. So we'll not discuss it further. I want you to take him out today, and make sure he gets set free by supper time." And with that she walked away, leaving Bobby miserable and muttering to himself. "It's not fair, it's just not fair."

But deep down, he knew that it was not fair to the fish any more. And his mother was right, he had agreed to release the fish one day. So he spent the rest of the day sitting in front of the aquarium, looking at Frankie. Frankie of course had no idea of what was happening or what was about to happen. He had grown quite comfortable in the tank, and had completely forgotten about his early days in the lake. But by supper time that was going to change.

As it grew nearer to 5:00pm, their usual supper time, Bobby's Mom reminded him about his task for the day. By that time, Bobby had resolved that there was nothing more he could do to change things, and he understood as well that the fish did need a bigger world. So off he went with Frankie, scooped up once again in the net. That really shocked the fish, he had no idea what was going on, except for the fact he did not like this suspended in air stuff. Since it was just a short distance to the lake, Frankie did not get too upset or out of breath. And when Bobby lowered the net into the lake, Frankie was flabbergasted! Bobby had not yet flipped the net over, he wanted to see the fish one last time and watched it swim around inside the net, bulging the sides out as it tried to escape.

"Well, Frankie" said Bobby "I guess this is it. You've been a really good fish and now I'm going to set you free." And with those words, Bobby flipped over the net and in a flash, the fish was gone.

Frankie dove deep, and then shot back up, leaping out of the water and doing a few somersaults. He couldn't believe that his head was not bumping against glass, that he had so much room to swim! And when he broke the surface and did those flips, Bobby saw how happy his fish was and realized how right his mother had been. Frankie grew ever larger in the coming weeks, and whenever he came near a fisherman's lure, he somehow knew that this was not food and was to be avoided. But he would often shoot out of the water, causing the fishermen to gape in wonder at the size of that bass. Regular fishermen would tell the tale of this fish that seemed almost to taunt them, and nobody was ever able to catch him. That fact made Bobby immensely proud, and he sometimes in future months would still see Frankie jumping in the air. Whenever he was lucky enough to see those jumps, he'd shout out in friendship

"Whoohoo Frankie! You keep growing fish."

So when your parents remind you about the importance of responsibility, caring and discipline, remember Frankie the fish!

Gordy the goldfinch

Gordy zigged in to the feeder. He dove sharply to land on the top left post. It was a maneuver easily accomplished when you had a clear path. But another, more aggressive little brother jumped up to block him. Gordy had to abandon his dive and veer off, cursing under his breath. Nothing nasty. He was just frustrated that he got beat again. It was not only his brothers who were beating him to the food. Neighbouring birds also were taking advantage of Gordy's laid back niceness and treating it like a weakness. Gordy was getting angrier and more moody. And that was starting to show, that was the worst part. The other birds were avoiding him. The more he thought about it, the more he had to agree. He was depressing to be around. Often complaining about things, instead of finding the sunlight. Gordy was receding into some kind of grayness. Not yet darkness, but that would happen too if he did not change, even just a little. Gordy was turning into a complainer, and nobody likes a complainer. A whiner. So how to change?

He sat on the juniper branch and weighed his options. "I could fight back and assert myself" he thought. But that would mean making enemies. And Gordy just did not have the confidence in his physical strength. Not yet any way. The physical strength is something he would have to develop over the long run. Muscles don't happen overnight. They take planning and time. Using muscles alone would make Gordy just like some of the other bully birds. Gordy needed to come at this problem from another angle.

One thing at which Gordy was very good was words. He had a fabulous vocabulary for such a young goldfinch. His Dad had instilled in Gordy a love of language. He would always share new words with Gordy whenever he came across them. And as Gordy grew older, he would also consult his Dad's thesaurus to find meanings and applications for new words.

But Gordy realized that he could not come flat out and insult his brothers and neighbours with words they did not understand. That was a sure-fire way to get scorned and picked on even more. "How can I make words work for me?" thought Gordy.

"Games! That's what all kids enjoy. Adults too but kids and games go hand in hand. "

And so Gordy set about to make up a word game. "Whenever somebody tries to push me around, I'll start a word game."

The next time Gordy got pushed away from the feeder he shouted out. "Bully! Who can give me a word that rhymes with bully?"

The other birds looked at him with amazement. "What do you mean bully? "

"Well come on" said Gordy. "If you don't want a reputation as a bully, then give me a word that rhymes."

"Why should we care what you think at all?" was the answer he got.

"Because sooner or later you're going to push a bigger bird and they will push back. I'm trying to help you guys out. Give you a bigger world picture. Learn how to express yourself in words or you will end up flat on your back. Is that where you want to end up? Flat on your back? Sure, you can push me around all you want, but I'm a lot smaller than you guys. Everybody out there is not going to be smaller. What will you do then if you can't communicate? I'll tell you what. You'll end up on your bum, lying in the grass wondering what hit you. So give me a word."

The other birds still did not understand the game. Gordy helped them out.

"Gully. Folly. Silly. Frilly. It's easy guys. Just let your imagination be your guide. The word doesn't have to rhyme exactly. Why can't you guys have a little fun instead of trying to be top dog all the time?"

"OK. How about stupid?" Said a big cowbird.

That drew laughter and back slaps from all the other bully birds. Gordy answered. ``Cupid.``

They all looked at him as if he was from some other planet. ``Cupid? How about Goopid?" responded cowbird.

"Now you're getting the hang of it" said Gordy. "Goopid isn't really a word, but that's a good start. Here's another one. "Seed."

Well that sparked some more ideas. "Bleed" said Bluejay. "Like what you're going to do when I smack you to the ground." And again the bully birds laughed. Gordy was determined to make some headway with his bird bully neighbours. "Very good" he said "That is an excellent rhyme. Let's keep it going. Need."

A huge raven piped in, "Feed. Which is what you will be soon." Again the others laughed and snorted. But they were responding. And that was at least a start. "Freed" said Gordy. "Who's next?"

The local cardinal chimed in with "Treed".

"Yes" shouted Gordy. "That's a good one. Treed. We're all treed."

"Weed" shouted the dove.

"Heed" said the starling

"Need" piped in chickadee.

And just like that, Gordy got them into a conversation. Very basic. Very short. But they were talking.

That is sometimes all it takes to get people of different backgrounds and interests to engage. Just some very basic and simple dialogue. Conversation. Communication.

So remember, whenever a difficult situation presents itself, one that you might normally think can only be solved by conflict and fighting, start a simple conversation. Before you know it, you'll be talking and discussing instead of fighting. Use words wisely and keep learning new words.

Harry the horse

Harry was one of the few remaining wild stallions still running free in the foothills of the Rockies. He was descended from a group of Spanish horses that came over to America with Cortez. Through the centuries they had developed into excellent climbers and had a much thicker coat of hair than one normally finds in ranch horses. These were truly mountain horses. But most had been caught up in man's relentless march westward, looking for more and more pasture for cattle. One by one they had been lassoed and "broken" into ranch horses. They were much prized by cowboys because of their surefooted confidence in the rugged terrain, and because they had a superior energy level relative to regular ranch horses. Harry, who rarely saw other wild horses, had developed a supreme ability to pick his way through rocky terrain. He was one of a kind and had managed thus far to avoid being captured by cowboys. It was not any kind of sixth sense that he had, in fact he was very curious. It was simply such a large area that he roamed in, and it had only recently been visited by cowboys and their cattle.

It was this very curiosity that was Harry's undoing on a wild and blustery October morning. Harry heard some strange sounds coming from over a ridge, and decided the unusual noise was worth investigating. He trotted up to the ridge and when he crested, what beheld his eyes was an extraordinary sight. There were at least 500 head of cattle being herded his way by six men on horses. They all saw Harry and one of the horsemen gave the order to go after Harry, leaving just two cowboys to mind the herd. Had Harry been closer to the rocky terrain he was used to, he likely would have got free. But he was at least 3 miles from the boulder patches and these cow horses could run as fast as he could in open terrain. Their cowboys were also expert at managing cattle and quickly spread out in a V formation, hoping to ensnare Harry before he got to his safe refuge. Harry almost made it, getting to within 300 metres of the rocks, but in his way were two cowboys on their mounts, lassos circling in the air. Harry felt the tug of rope on his neck and that was it. He was caught. He bucked and jumped, twisting and turning, causing one of the cowboys to severely sprain his ankle as he held on. But there was no escaping. Harry was led back to the cattle herd where the lead hand marveled at his stature.

"Now that is one beautiful horse" said the hand. His companions all muttered in approval. "Damn frisky though I'll tell you that. It'll be a long time breaking this one. He damn near tore my hand off!" cursed the cowboy with the sprained hand.

They made sure Harry was securely tied to a stake, and bunked in for the evening as tomorrow would be a long cattle drive back to the ranch house. They were eager to get back for some real home cooking, having been living on beans and salted meat for several weeks. Harry was so tired from the days ordeal that he also closed his eyes and dropped to sleep.

The next morning found Harry wide awake before any of the cattlemen had stirred from their sleeping rolls. He started to whinny and snort and kick. This woke the ranchers who cursed and muttered again. "That horse is going to be nothing but trouble. I sure do not want to waste my time breaking him" said the lead hand. So they gathered their gear, made sure Harry was tied securely with two loops around his neck (which Harry valiantly tried to shake off) and they all saddled up and headed back to the ranch. It was a 4 hours canter, all were eager to push the pace and get back. They arrived shortly before noon, and led Harry directly to a corral. He started pacing around, furious that he was locked in. His entire life had been filled with freedom, and now he was locked in a circle.

One of the ranchers approached him with some more rope. Harry, unlike any other horse they had dealt with, charged directly at the rancher. He dropped his rope and jumped over the railing, barely beating a solid head butt from Harry. "That is one mean horse. I'm not going near it. Let the boss try if he wants." But the ranch boss was a few days ride away, attending to some other matters. So Harry would not be bothered further that day.

The next morning, after Harry had eaten some of the oats laid out for him, he noticed a young boy watching him from behind the barn. It was Zachary, the rancher's son. He had heard about the new stallion and wanted to see for himself if this horse was indeed as wild as the ranch hands had described. "Well" said Zachary "You certainly don't seem like a crazy horse. In fact you look pretty darn handsome." His words were soothing to Harry. Unlike the ranchers, he did not perceive a threat from this boy. But, his experience over the past several days had shown him that these humans were unlikely to be friendly. So he remained where he was and watched the young lad.

Zachary opened the corral gate slowly, and walked inside the enclosure. He purposely did not take a rope, understanding that it would only be interpreted instinctively by the horse as a threat. He was right. Harry watched him as he stood there. Zachary watched back. Neither one of them moved. Even though he was just a young lad, Zachary had learned that horses, be they wild or ranch horses, did not enjoy having stuff on their backs or around their necks. It just made sense. Who wants to be tied up? That's just crazy.

So, after a few minutes checking each other out, Zachary started to walk around the perimeter of the corral. He did not encroach on the horse's space, and stopped walking as soon as the horse would make a move to back away. Harry found this approach to be quite unusual; in fact, he even dared think that this young human was respecting him. And after a good hour of this back and forth activity, Zachary began to tighten the circle. Harry let him come in closer. Zachary was careful as well, to keep his head down, only looking up directly at the horse every few minutes. After some time, he got within arm's reach of Harry. He stopped. Harry stopped. They both raised their heads and looked at each other. Right in the eyes. Zachary smiled. Harry smiled. Zachary slowly raised his right arm to within inches of Harry's nose. And he let Harry come forward to touch his hand. So formed their connection. And within 15 minutes, Zachary was riding the horse bareback around the corral.

The next morning, the ranch hands could not believe their eyes when they came out from the kitchen after their morning grub. Nor could Zachary's dad who had returned the night prior from his ranch duties. Harry was riding the horse bareback around and around in circles. And he would occasionally stop and stroke the horse's neck. Harry snorted in delight at this. Zachary's dad marveled at this and said "Son, if you can break this crazy horse and I see with my own eyes that you have, then you are ready to join us in the mountains. We ride out tomorrow son. You better get this horse used to wearing a saddle." And so Zachary did. They rode out with all the ranch hands the next day, receiving hearty slaps on the back in congratulations. And Harry reveled in the praise as well; he somehow knew that his life had turned for the better with this boy.

Acts of kindness can bring great dividends.

Inta the iguana

Today started like just about every other day for Inta the iguana. The howler monkeys were the first to arise in the jungle, and their territorial barking woke up the rest of the forest creatures. "Those darned monkeys" Inta protested, as she tried to get another few minutes of shut eye. But there was no sleeping in today. There were several troops of monkeys in the area, all vying for their food source, so the racket was quite loud indeed. "If I see those monkeys today I will give them a piece of my mind" she exclaimed. Not that it would do any good, the monkeys always laughed at everybody's protests. They were quite insensitive to everybody's needs but their own.

Inta gave her mom and dad a big kiss and started her way down the branch. She passed Uncle Larry along the way, he was in no hurry to forage for food and lay draped over the branch, all four legs hanging comfortably down like some massive roots. Larry was quite large for an iguana, and everybody wondered how that could be since hardly anybody ever saw him eating! "Hi, Uncle Larry. Can I step over you or will you move just a little bit so I can get by" laughed Inta. Larry grunted and shifted his position a tad so she could squeeze by. "Thanks Uncle Larry. Have a nice day" she whistled on her way past. Larry gave her another grunt. Strangers might think him very rude, but Inta knew uncle Larry loved her as much as her own mom and dad. He was just kind of lazy.

Inta scoured the trunk and branches of their tree but it had been picked quite clean of insects, at least the big ones that she enjoyed so much. If she was super hungry at the end of the day she would stop to flick the tiny ones, but it was too early to spend time doing that. She wanted a big breakfast. So off she went along the forest floor, heading for some new trees she had not yet scoured. Iguanas do not like to scamper on the forest floor for too long; it is not their natural habitat. They like it up in the trees or along shrubs. Inta had moved along for about 10 minutes when she saw what she guessed would be a rich breakfast tree. It was massive. Close to ten ft in diameter. It stretched high up into the forest canopy and was carpeted with epiphytes. She giggled with delight at her find. She could spend all morning here and get her fill for the whole day. "Hooray, hooray! I'll be so full by noon I will barely be able to get back to our home tree."

So up the tree she went. Stopping every now and then to gorge on the cicadas and beetles that didn't know what hit them. What hit them was a long and very accurate iguana tongue. Inta was having so much fun she did not realize what was happening below her. A strange two legged creature (strange to Inta when she finally did see it too late since she had not yet seen any humans) was following Inta's progress up the tree. The human had been drawn to this part of the jungle by the howling of the monkeys and he was armed with the latest technology. He had binoculars, burlap sacks, tie wraps and something very dangerous to all animals, a rifle loaded with nerve darts. These could immobilize just about any animal for several minutes. Enough time for the poacher to grab the animal, tie its legs with the plastic wraps and stuff it into his sack. He had not used his nerve darts on iguanas before, and since he had not yet seen any monkeys he thought he'd give it a try. He slowly shouldered his rifle and sighted onto Inta. It was poor Inta this time who did not know what hit her. She felt a pinch in her bum and snapped around to see what had bit her. She had not noticed anything dangerous or even irritating on her way up the tree, so she was quite startled at what greeted her. A funny fluffy thing with multiple colours was sticking in her bum. She had never seen the likes of it before, and as she craned her neck to try and nip it out of her skin, her vision got very blurry and at at the same time she felt really woozy.

"What could this be?" was the last thing she remembered before waking an hour later. Here is what happened in that hour. An instant after feeling woozy, Inta toppled from her perch and fell to the ground. Thankfully she was completely limp when she fell, or her neck would probably have snapped. She fell a good thirty feet and landed almost at the poacher's feet. He quickly secured her legs with his plastic wrap and scooped her into one of his sacks. "Now this will fetch me a pretty penny" he said. The poacher had spent the next thirty minutes looking for the howler monkeys but lucky for them, he did not find any. And so he headed out of the jungle.

When Inta came to, she couldn't move any of her legs, they were all tied together. Try as she might, she could just wiggle her claws a little. And her body was all squished up inside the sack. She of course had no idea, where she was , but she knew that she was in big trouble. After an hour of this jostling in the sack, being moved from one shoulder of the poacher to another, she was dropped to the ground. "Oww, now that hurt!" she shouted, but the poacher could not hear her. Only some other animals nearby, also in sacks could understand.

"Hey you, what are you?" she heard from somebody who seemed to be right next to her, but in another sack. "I'm an iguana, what are you and what is this place?" "I'm a scarlet macaw and we've been poached!" "What is poached?" asked Inta, quite new to this concept. "Oh boy, are you in for a nasty surprise" said the macaw. "We've been stolen from our forest by a human and I've heard that what happens next can be very frightening."

"What happens next?" asked Inta.

"Well, we may find ourselves locked up in a house with bars" replied the macaw, "And I've even heard that birds lose their ability to fly, so I can't imagine what they will do to you."

"Oh my goodness" replied Inta. "Is this true?"

"Of course it is true" said the macaw. " I heard it from a big old scarlet who actually escaped before they could clip his wings."

Before she could respond, Inta felt herself being lifted up, and then unceremoniously dumped onto a cement floor. She blinked her eyes several times before she got used to the light. And what beheld her was indeed a sorry sight. There were several forest creatures around her, all tied up as well. The macaw she had been speaking with, a couple of green parrots, 3 tiny little forest tigers who couldn't be more than 8 weeks old, and one pesquite who was howling and squealing in fear.

The poacher grabbed Inta by her tail and hoisted her into a box. The box had a few holes drilled into it, and before she could squirm into a more comfortable position, a lid was nailed shut over top of her. The only light that came in was thru the tiny air holes. "Funny" she thought " I'm so glad I have a full belly." And indeed it was. Because Inta would not see any food again for at least 48 hours! The next two days found her traveling in trucks and cars. And at one time she was even strapped to the back of a motorcycle. They were headed to Puerto Armuelles by the ocean, where the poacher hoped to sell all the animals to middlemen who then found collectors around the world. All very illegal and horrible, but very real.

When they arrived at the port, it was late in the day, and the poacher stopped at a cafe for some dinner. He left all the animals stacked outside in boxes. Passersby and other diners did not give it much thought because this kind of activity apparently happened regularly. But one diner took notice. His name was Arthur, and he had traveled from Canada to go on an extended jungle hike with his Costa Rican buddy Francisco. Not speaking much Spanish, he asked Francisco to inquire what the boxes contained. Being a local, Francisco knew right away they were poached animals destined for illegal sale. "That's awful" said Arthur. "Surely these people have other ways to make money?" But work was hard to come by in this remote part of the world, and Francisco explained that even though he did not approve either, people still had to put food on their tables and provide for their families.

"Well let's do something to help both the people and the animals" said Arthur. "Ask him how much he wants for all the animals".

Francisco could not believe his ears. "You wish to buy all the boxes?!"

"Yes, every one of them" replied Arthur. "Go ahead, make him a proposal."

So Francisco approached the poacher who guffawed and shouted out a ridiculous amount of money.

"Tell him I will pay him half of what he asks" said Arthur. That still amounted to almost one month's wages for most workers in this area. "Go ahead, tell him."

And so Francisco offered the man US $150 for all the animals. "Loco" is what Arthur heard, but he smiled. He knew that amount would not be turned down. It was possible the poacher would get more from middlemen, but it was too attractive and easy a sale to pass up. No need to cart the boxes any further or engage in exhausting negotiations with middlemen. And so he pocketed the $150 and left the restaurant.

Now Arthur had 6 boxes of various jungle species. He looked at his friend and said "Francisco, tonight we are going to liberate all these animals." And that is exactly what they did. They rented a taxi, piled all the boxes in the trunk, and paid the driver to take them as far as he could down the dirt path that wound its way out of Pto Armuelles and into the jungle. At the end of the road, they placed all the boxes at the side of the road where the jungle was thickest, opened them all, and stared in amazement at the various species. Inta the iguana, small tigers, macaws, pesquites, even a sloth!

They backed away and watched as each animal climbed out of its box and hurried away into the dense jungle. Inta was the last to leave. She gasped at this turn of events, not comprehending what had just happened. But she knew that something incredible had just happened because here she was, on the doorstep of the jungle. Strange environment and not her own home, but the trees smelled similar and off she went to find herself a new home. Free. It was her lucky day that Arthur had decided to also stop for dinner at the same diner as her captor the poacher. Just plain good luck.

41

Luck can change things for the better, even when you have almost given up hope. Never give up hope.

Jeremy the jackal

There is an African expression well known to many. Hakuna Matata. It means "No problem". This was not however a widely used phrase in the jackal community. Being the scavengers that they are, a "no problem" mentality would not get food into your belly nor feed your family. Jackals were constantly on the lookout for food, and if they were fortunate enough to find a carcass, it invariably was the skin and bone they got to pick over. Lions and other predators higher up the food chain would have first go at any fresh meat. Even vultures would often get at stinky carcasses before the jackal. The jackal's life was a constant battle. Either with other animals, or with each other. And if there was nothing to scavenge they had to then plan attacks on weaker animals, be it a young gazelle or sick water buffalo. These attacks had to be well coordinated and stealthily accomplished. And therein lay the problem. Stealth. It was not one of Jeremy's strongest qualities. In fact, poor Jeremy was about the loudest of jackals ever to patrol the savannah.

All jackals have a cackle, a nasty sounding laugh. But Jeremy's was particularly shrill. It could be described as a combination chain saw and steam whistle blasting together. And not only was the sound outrageous and loud, poor Jeremy had little control over when and where he let loose with it. He had somehow missed the early years development when jackals all learned how to hunt. Well, not missed it exactly. Jeremy had gone to hunting class with all the other young jackals, he simply failed to get the concept of stealth and its importance in hunting. Not really his fault at all. Whenever he opened his mouth, the wildest sounds would emanate. It was such a disturbing sound that his fellow jackal den mates would cringe and slink away, all very embarrassed for Jeremy. Not to mention very annoyed at losing their train of thought whilst hunting.

Whenever the jackals did achieve a successful hunt, usually with Jeremy absent, by the time Jeremy arrived on the scene there was barely anything left, save for white bones. So Jeremy was gradually wasting away, getting thinner and thinner. His ribs were pushing out against his mangy fur. His legs looked like knobby twigs. Hunting on his own was completely out of the question. He could hardly stumble a few paces before collapsing to the ground. In a word, Jeremy was dying.

But through all this disappearing body mass, his voice remained as strong and irritating as ever. And as things turned out, that buzz saw whistle would be his saving grace.

One beautiful star lit night, with meteors shooting through the sky, the pack was sound asleep in their den, having feasted all day on the remains of a gazelle carcass that had for some strange reason been left almost untouched by the cheetah who had brought it down. Who knows why he had hardly touched a mouthful? Perhaps the sleek cat had been frightened away by some bigger animal. Or perhaps it was just nature's way of providing for the jackals in times of need. Whatever the reason, they had finally gotten a full meal and were so completely satiated from their feast, they did not hear nor recognize a serious danger that was approaching their lair. Lions.

The kings of the African savannah were on a night hunt and had not found any success until one of them sensed the strong and pungent odor of the jackals. The lions felt no qualms about lowering their usual high standards and eating jackal if that was all there was to be had. So they got nearer and nearer to the jackals lair. Still no alarm was sounded. All the jackals were snoring contentedly, bellies full, jaws sore from their afternoon gazelle buffet. All except for one. Jeremy.

Jeremy had not eaten for several days. He had simply fallen onto a patch of soft savannah grass a short distance from the lair, hopeful that one of his pack would take pity on him and bring him some leftovers from the gazelle. But times were tough for everybody, as evidenced by the lions now hunting jackal. So Jeremy's health was not even on the radar of the other jackals.

When Jeremy saw the lions approaching his pack's den, he at first concluded that this was simply a hallucination brought on by his extreme hunger. But the clear night sky and full moon made the scene abundantly clear to Jeremy. He was not imagining this. The lions were going to attack his pack and very possibly make mincemeat of them all.

Jeremy did what he did best. He let out a blood curdling series of shrieks and howls that even made the lions stop dead in their tracks, stupefied as to what could generate such a horrendous sound. The entire pack jumped up and took on a howling and shrieking that echoed out the front of the lair, magnified by the walls that flared out like a trumpet. It was such a sound that the lions eardrums reverberated to such an extent, it was painful for them to stay where they were. So the entire pride turned tail and ran down the hillside to escape the noise and the pain. As the lions retreated, one lone voice continued to shrilly pierce the night air. Jeremy's distinctive shriek rang out louder than all the others. The jackals looked at each other in amazement. That scrawny little noisemaker had saved them all.

They all went out and joyously surrounded Jeremy, howling and shrieking with pleasure. Jeremy was ushered back to the lair, supported by his pack mates, and helped to lay down on a fresh patch of soft grass near the entrance. He was lathered with thankful tongue caresses and head butts. And he fell into a very satisfying sleep, to awaken the next morning to a feast of freshly hunted savannah critters. Rabbits and gophers and whatever else the pack rousted out the previous night. For many of them had stayed up all night hunting for Jeremy. Jeremy grew stronger by the day, always with something to eat no matter how meager the pickings were for his lair mates. They always made sure Jeremy had enough food. For he was now the alarm bell that sounded whenever the lair was threatened by bigger and stronger hunters. Never again was the lair subjected to an ambush. Nothing got too close before Jeremy let out his howls and shrieks to frighten away all creatures that posed any threat to the jackals.

Voice is a powerful tool. Recognize what yours can and cannot do for you.

Korry the koala

In the middle of Australia a young koala named Korry was trying to reach the most tender of eucalyptus leaves high in the tree. He was stretching and stretching, barely hanging onto the branch. Koalas are great climbers, and can hang onto the smallest of branches but even they are subject to the laws of gravity. And sure enough, the branch could only bend so much and snapped, sending Korry tumbling to the ground. The Australian summer drought had fortunately drained most of the water from the branches so they were tinder dry and snapped easily as Korry fell. Had this been the rainy season he would surely have broken his back before hitting the ground.

At least the tip of the eucalyptus branch had also fallen with Korry. It lay draped over his chest. Korry's breathing was at first, on impact with the ground, very fast. But the fall had knocked him out cold, and soon enough his body slowed down as did his breathing. He remained unconscious and he lay there on the barren and dry soil. No broken bones, but definitely concussed. Thankfully it was the height of day, and with the massive heat, most animals remained quite still, either sleeping or in shade, waiting for night. Especially the predators. Packs of dingos roamed this part of the desert but none were to be seen or heard at this time. As night started to creep into the scene, Korry lay motionless, breathing but not moving. It was not until three hours later, when the black of the Australian desert night had overtaken the landscape that Korry opened his eyes.

"Oh Lord, let me please move my toes" he gasped. And Korry wiggled his toes.

"Thank you Lord for saving me. But what shall become of me now?" he asked.

For the fall had knocked some of his memory into another part of his brain, inaccessible for now. Korry had no idea where he was. In reality he was just a few minutes from his mother's den, but Korry had no idea. As his eyes adjusted to the darkness of night, he began to notice some shapes. A distant mountain. Nearby rolling hills and lots and lots of sand. Rock. Very little vegetation, except for the stand of eucalyptus where he had fallen. Nothing looked familiar. "I don't know this place. How could I not know this place?" he asked. "Why, I cannot even remember how I got here."

But the eucalyptus branch, the fact it was freshly broken, started to stir at least some memory.

"Ah, yes" he thought. "I must have been climbing this tree." A sensible deduction of course, but it did not help any with his orientation.

"There must be some way to figure out where I am." Slowly beginning to understand his predicament. Out in the wild alone. No light. No sense of where he was.

Well, just picture how you would feel if you were in Korry's shoes. Uhh...claws. You're lost and alone and the night is not yet a place in which you are comfortable. So the more he fretted over this, the faster his heart beat and the less secure he felt.

"I must go higher to see if anything is familiar" he told himself. "Walk to the foothills and see what you can see".

So off he went, as fast as his sloth legs and hands could carry him. Tumbling along with his head down, occasionally bringing it up to make sure he was on the right track. Scrape and jump. Pump and run. He kept a pretty good pace for a sloth. And the fact he was a little scared served to give him more speed than one would normally see in a sloth. They are not used to being on the ground, especially at night.

Korry made it to the start of the foothills, and climbed higher. He was able to take advantage of some trees and even made like a monkey, swinging from one to another. He finally made it up to the highest part

47

of the foothills and climbed the tallest tree. But it was so dark he could not see very far. So he decided to stay up in the tree and rest until the morning sun came. Korry fell fast asleep.

He was awakened in the early morning by the loud barking and yelling of some howler monkeys. The sun was rising over the horizon. Its warm glow started to bathe the surrounding countryside in light. And as Korry's eyes adjusted to the daylight, he climbed even higher up in the tree. As he neared the top, the sound of the howler monkeys bounced off the foothills. And then Korry saw what he had been hoping to see. Far off in the distance was the green lake he knew from his childhood days. It was there that his mother had brought Korry and his brothers and sisters for a daily drink and swim.

"So that is where I must head" he said to himself. And from high up where he sat, Korry could see that there were no predators for miles around. "If I get a good start now, I can be home before night falls again." And down he climbed, heading off in the direction of his home. Korry did make it home to shouts of joy and laughter from his family and friends.

What had Korry learned from his adventure? He would always remember that the high ground was a safe place to be. Never go running at night if you don't know where you are. Climb to high ground and figure out where you have to go before you make your move. And wait for daylight when you are in a strange place.

When you are afraid take a deep breath and slow down. Never panic.

Louie the lion

Although Louie was the biggest lion in his class, he was certainly not the smartest. It would not be fair to call Louie dumb. He was just bored. Being so large can make a lion lazy. Louie's size often got him what he wanted. And when there is not much effort in achieving what you want, life can get quite boring. Boredom was driving Louie crazy. He needed an adventure. So one day he told his buddies he was going to skip class and go hunting on his own.

"Don't do it" said his friends. "You're not good enough yet to hunt on your own, and besides, skipping class will get you in trouble."

"Then trouble is what I'll get" replied Louie. "I can't sit here another day and go over the same lessons again and again. It's boring me to death!"

"Louie" said Bob, his closest buddy, "You're bored because you don't pay attention in class and you have to keep repeating things. Pay attention and maybe you would not have to repeat things so much. And frankly Louie, being in class is better than being in jail!"

That was especially true for Louie, even though he was not yet smart enough to understand it. Instead of questioning authority, Louie would reject it outright. That's pretty common for some lions of his age. And I suppose it has a lot to do with effort and patience. It takes work to think rationally and interpret stuff. A lot easier when you are young, to simply discard and do.

But Louie would not listen. When the lunch bell sounded he sneaked out the back of the school and headed for the savannah.

He bounded over the tall grass, leaping 10 ft with each stride. Louie was possessed of a free energy that knew no bounds. Within minutes he was out of sight of the school and surrounded by the raw plains of his ancestors. Banyan trees lined the edge of the Jacomo river where he finally decided to pause and hydrate. His giant tongue lapped at the gently moving waters of Jacomo. Louie filled his tank before looking up. What caught his eye made him crouch low to the ground. Frozen. A solitary wildebeest was drinking on the other side of the river. Not a large beast, likely no more than 200 lbs. Louie guessed it was about 2 years old. And completely oblivious to Louie's presence. The wildebeest would occasionally lift his head and scan Louie's side of the river, but it did not register Louie's presence. The drought had made even the most skittish of animals less cautious. And wildebeests were normally like tightly strung rubber bands, ready to snap at the slightest movement.

"Must be a serious vision problem" thought Louie. "Good thing the wind is at his back and not mine."

Now the river was quite shallow at this point. Louie guessed that at its deepest his belly would still be clear of the water. "If I make my move when his head is down that will give me at least a couple seconds head start before he even moves" mused Louie. "If my first jump is strong enough I can whack that guy before he gets up the other bank."

And so Louie jumped. Water exploded into the air. The wildebeest instinctively jumped back. But so startled was it, that it's first step was a breaking stumble and it fell head first into the river muck. Louie was halfway across the stream. The wildebeest struggled mightily and freed himself from the muck. It bounded toward the bank. Legs springing into motion. Pistons driving the earth. But before it had reached the base of the bank, Louie was on the shore. His eyes on fire. He could taste the meal to come. He also sprang forward, closing the gap between himself and the beast with alarming speed. Alarming for the wildebeest that is.

Just as the wildebeest was about to mount the crest, a mass of black hair appeared at the lip, stretching at least 50 metres on either side of the wildebeest. It was the rest of his herd! They heard the commotion and lunged forward toward the river, in unison, like a flock of birds. They crashed over the river back and bowled Louie over. He tumbled backward to the edge of the river, bruised and battered as the herd's momentum drove forward.

And then, as if they had magnetically been pulled back by some powerful force, they turned around and crashed back to the bank. Louie was left with his mouth wide open, panting and in pain. His chest heaved. "Likely a couple of broken ribs" he muttered. What the hey just happened?" he shouted out. He had not energy to follow the herd, nor would that have been smart given the herd's size.

And as Louie turned to look at his side of the river the reason for the wildebeest's spontaneous turn around became apparent. His buddies from school were standing at the lip of the river bank. A majestic line of lions. Eight of them. Mouths still wide open, their ear splitting roar reverberating between the riverbanks.

"So that's what happened!' shouted Louie. "Hey guys, am I ever glad you showed up. I thought I was a goner."

"You would have been, you big lummox" replied one of the pride. "I'm telling you. There's gonna be a day when you'll be too far away, and we won't have your back anymore."

"I get it." responded Louie. "I really get it now. I'm gonna listen a little more from now on."

And with that final comment they all turned and headed back to school. Louie caught up and repeated "No. I'm really serious now. That was too close for comfort. I really do see the power of the pride. Thanks guys."

Look out for your friends.

Morton the monkey

The Amazon River is a mighty powerful river. It can change its course, its depth, and many an animal has been caught by its changes. Morton the monkey was one animal who was soon to find out about the power of the Amazon.

Morton lived in the wildest and remotest past of the amazon, deep in the Brazilian rain forest. He had grown up there with his tribe and learned all about the river from his elders. Like most monkeys, Morton's tribe spent their days in the trees. They looked for tasty leaves and fruit and nuts. And a good part of their day was also spent grooming each other. That's the thing about monkeys. Their personal hygiene is totally for the birds, so they rely on each other to take care of their grooming. A pretty good system actually, if you're not too big on bathing and brushing your teeth!

Well this day had started out much like any other for Morton. Up at the crack of dawn. Not because it was dawn, but because the older monkeys raised such a fierce racket in the morning. They delighted in blasting out their vocal chords as loud as they could. It was like some kind of competition amongst them. Who could make the loudest sounds! Morton thought it was really very silly, so he skedaddled out of the tree and vine jumped his way a few trees over. His buddies were already there, waiting for him "Where ya been sleepy head?" his buddy Anton asked. Anton and Morton were just about best buddies. Same age, give or take a few days. They did everything together. And so it was today they would go looking for food together. "Aw, you know how it is" replied Morton "If I could get any extra sleep in, you guys wouldn't see me for hours. But now my brother is starting to bark away in the morning too. Bad enough that the others do, but he's right next to me so as soon as he starts I'm outta there!" "Yeah, I don't quite get that part of being a monkey you know?" replied Jeremy.

So off they went, along with two other buddies, happily swinging thru the trees, trying to outdo each other with their balance and moves. Every now and then one of them would slip and tumble, but not too far. Monkeys are great at catching a limb and breaking their fall. It made for some good whooping and hollering though. They were having a blast. This went on for a good hour, until one of them said "Hey guys, don't you think we should be maybe getting a bit to eat?" In all their exuberance, they had completely forgotten about breakfast! "Yessiree" said Morton "I'm so hungry I could eat a papaya!"

Their swinging turned to more of a scouting mission, each vying with the other to see who would be the first to find that tasty tree. There was no prize attached to being first, other than bragging rights like it is with all kids. It did not take long for one of them to signal that the prize had been found. Jeremy shouted out "Check this out guys, a huge mango tree that hasn't been touched yet!" Sure enough, Jeremy had found a very large mango tree, filled with the ripest and juiciest mangoes any of them had seen for quite some time. "All right!" yelled Morton. "You are the definite winner today!" And they all scampered over to the tree and started to gorge on the mangoes. It does not take long to fill a little monkey's tummy, and soon they were all crashed out on various limbs, looking more like sloths than monkeys, their tails curled around a branch for security, arms dangling. "That was some feast" said Morton, to nobody in particular. They all nodded their heads in approval as one by one they dozed off, none of them having any further energy to eat or move further.

A loud crack of lighting roused them up, and the skies above turned gray and black. "We better get back home" said Jeremy. "You know how the river can change really fast, and there is that open section that we have to get across." All except Morton shook themselves awake and headed back.

"Hey Morton" said Jeremy "Aren't you coming?" Morton said "I'm just going to go a little further up and get a few more juicy mangoes. This kind of tree doesn't come along every day."

Jeremy nodded in agreement. "But don't be long man, you know what will happen if you get caught on the wrong side of the river."

"Yeah, yeah, don't worry I'll be but a few minutes behind you guys." laughed Morton.

So off they went, and up Morton went. Higher and higher to the very tip of the mango tree, where he figured the sun's rays would have ripened some really tasty mangoes. He was right. Near the top of the tree were some bright orange and red mangoes, some of them actually dripping with juice. "Pay day " thought Morton. I'm gonna get me some of those beauties." He proceeded again to gorge himself. You know what happens when monkeys gorge themselves. As happened with he and his buddies earlier, Morton felt very sleepy. "I'll just have a quick nap and then be on my way" he thought. And he draped himself over a branch and snoozed off almost immediately.

And as he was underneath some other leaf laden branches, he did not feel the rain as it started to get heavier and heavier. Soon the clouds had opened up, and the rain was pounding down, a veritable tropical storm. But Morton snoozed on, oblivious to the cascading waterfalls around him and the quickly expanding Amazon river. In no time at all, the ground below the tree was covered in a few inches of water and it kept on rising. By the time Morton roused himself from his slumber, the Amazon had grown to completely engulf the surrounding lands, and it kept on coming. "Oh, no" cried Morton. "This is going to be a big problem." And he started to swing his way back thru the trees, blinking his eyes every few seconds to clear the rain. It did not take long to get to the crossing, but as he had feared, the Amazon had risen about 8 feet in that short span of time. What had before been a relatively easy river crossing, jumping from branch to branch and occasionally scampering thru shallow water, was now an impossibly wide expanse of fast moving water. "How am I going to manage this" thought Morton.

He sat in the tree nearest to the river and mulled over his options. Well, option really. He only had one. He would have to swim! But monkeys can't swim! At least, none had been known to swim before. "I'm just going to have to do it" thought Morton. Because the longer he waited, the higher the river rose.

And so Morton proceeded cautiously down the tree trunk, inching closer and closer to the river. He was not at all clear on how things would proceed, but he did know that staying put was not an option. If the river kept rising, as it appeared that it would, other animals would be driven to higher ground. And other reptiles, meaning anacondas and pythons. He would have no chance against them if caught in a single tree. And so he dipped his toe in the water, then slowly lowered his leg in, and bit by bit he slipped his body in, until only one hand was hanging on to the tree. "So this is it" he thought. "I can hang on here until something gets me or the river gets me, or I let go and see what happens."

So he let go. And to his utter astonishment, he floated! As he floated, he found that if he moved his arms and legs he could adjust where he was going. So with some basic paddling, and a little kicking, Morton found himself swimming! He was not yet out of danger, as the current was quite strong and carried him further downriver than he had been before. But with some more energetic kicking and moving of his arms, Morton found in a few minutes that his feet were touching bottom. He had made it to the other side! And so he kicked his way onto dry land, what little there was of it, and found a big tree to start his trek home.

It took about half an hour to get back to his home, and the other monkeys greeted him with whoops of joy. They thought he was a goner for sure! "I swam" yelled Morton, "I really swam across the river!" This proclamation was greeted with derisive grunts and yells. "Monkeys can't swim" they all shouted in unison! "But I did" said Morton. "How else do you think I made it across the river?!?" Now that gave pause for thought, because they all knew there was no dry crossing of the Amazon during a deluge like this one. But none would give him a chance to explain further, they all turned and went back to their perches to sit out the rain. All except for his mother. "Morton honey, I believe you. But just to be sure before you tell the others more, why don't you show me in the

morning after you get a good night's sleep. You must be exhausted."
Now that sounded just fine to Morton, he was exhausted. So he fell fast
asleep in his mother's arms and slept soundly thru the night, even with
the rain sounding like machine gun fire all around them. Morton was
safe and dry in his mother's arms.

And in the morning, before the others had a chance to awake,
Morton's mother gently shook him and said "Come on honey, let's go
down to the river and you can show me how to swim." Morton was still
kind of dozy, but he followed his mother to the river. "So this is how I did
it." And he dipped a toe in just like the night before. Then his hand, arm
and so on until he was up to his neck in water. "Oh Morton, do be
careful" cried his mother, not knowing 100% whether he could do it, and
also just showing her mother's concerns. But Morton gave her a wink,
and pushed off the shore into the current. He moved his arms and legs,
and swam in circles for his mother! She gasped with pleasure and
shouted for the other monkeys to come and see.

And that is how Morton and all the other monkeys in his tribe
learned how to swim!

Strange and exceptional circumstances can unleash hidden skills
and creativity.

Nancy the narwhal

Everybody has heard of blue whales, sperm whales, beluga whales, but not many people know about narwhals. Narwhals have the long ivory horn and have been called the unicorns of the ocean. Like a unicorn, a narwhal is supposed to bring good luck to whoever sees one. And they are not easy to spot as they are very shy creatures. Especially Nancy.

Nancy grew up in the far north of Canada. And I mean faaaar north! There were no human communities near to her favorite fishing grounds. Nancy did most of her swimming north of Hudson's Bay in a small bay called Tukyatuk. It was at the entrance to the Northwest Passage, a maritime route that was seeing more sea traffic as the polar ice kept melting. Nancy had managed to avoid the huge icebreakers. She could hear their grinding sound from miles away and would retreat into her special bay until the ships passed. It was a very solitary life, rarely seeing other mammals or humans, but it suited Nancy just fine. In fact, in her 4 years roaming the bay and surrounding sea, she had never seen any humans. Until one fine summer day last year.

The sun was shining. A slight north wind was blowing onto the land, barely causing a ripple on the water. The currents had brought a large school of sardines into the bay and that in turn attracted a large flock of terns easily visible from underwater. Nancy had learned to scan the sky for signs of activity, knowing that large groups of birds usually meant fish in the water. The local Inuit (an indigenous group of people who have lived in Canada's north for probably thousands of years) had also learned this trick. A group of Inuit hunters saw the circling terns and headed their kayaks to the area. They were whale and seal hunting!

The Inuit were still a good half hour away from arriving at the destination the terns had marked, and Nancy being a solo swimmer was unaware of their approach. She came up to the surface and gulped a mouthful of sardines. Sardines like to swim near the surface on sunny days; they enjoy the warmer water and the better visibility for finding their food source of plankton. So for the time being, everybody (except the sardines that Nancy and the terns caught!) was happy. Nancy was getting her fill of sardines, the school of sardines was feasting on plankton and the terns were dive bombing from above. It was a regular northern feast. There were no seals today as they were swimming under a pack of ice and had not seen the circling terns.

The Inuit knew their paddling would be masked by all this noise in the water. They also knew that there was bound to be good hunting wherever the terns were. They picked up their pace and went shooting thru the arctic waters, leaving ribbons of bubbles behind them. Swish. Swoosh. The paddles cut through the water like sharp knives. Nancy kept eating. So busy was she and so careless, that her narwhal tusk would break the water surface every time she swam up to grab a mouthful. The Inuit hunters saw this and signaled each other to widen their approach in a classic pincer maneuver. They were now whale hunting. Hunting Nancy.

All this noise from the feeding frenzy had alerted some other animals. Big animals. A blue whale. Blue whales have the most amazing hearing. Some scientists think they can hear underwater sounds hundreds of miles away. If that is true, then this particular blue must have a serious pounding in its head. It was just a few miles away from the school of sardines, having picked up their presence on its sonar. It knew there was good feeding here without having to see the flying terns. And its hearing was so good it also detected the paddle swishes of the hunters. Blue whales are very smart undersea creatures, and this one had survived for decades. It understood the danger that Inuit hunters presented. It also knew that another very loud undersea mammal, that being Nancy, was making a terrific racket. It put two and two together and concluded that the narwhal did not have a clue what fate might befall it.

So with a few powerful strokes of its tail, it was within visual range of all the activity. Nancy shooting to the surface with her mouth wide open. The swirling school of sardines. The dive bombing terns. And most importantly, the Inuit kayaks fast closing on the school and Nancy. The blue let out a massively loud blast that reverberated underwater for miles. Nancy heard it loud and clear. And she understood that was a danger signal from a fellow undersea creature. So she instinctively dove down. Not a second too late as the Inuit in the lead kayak had his harpoon in his hand, and was just about to launch it at Nancy. She dove deeper and deeper, in a panic. The blue caught up to her and guided her away from the scene to safer waters. And then the blue gently edged her upward, knowing that Nancy had reached her dive limit and was in danger of blowing up her lungs. As they got closer to the surface the blue told Nancy to wait as she surfaced to get a better view of the surroundings. The kayak hunters were far, far away, well out of range and knew they had been beaten this day.

Nancy was in tears, knowing that the big blue had saved her life. And it left Nancy with words of wisdom. "You had best go a little further south and find some companions with whom you can swim and hunt in safety. Even I meet up with my blue companions from time to time. It's OK to be alone for a while, but don't live alone forever. We all need companions."

And so she did. Nancy would remember this day for the rest of her life, and she always made a point of telling the story to any young narwhals she met along the way. The day big blue saved her life.

It's OK to be alone for a while, but don't be alone forever.

Ophelia the orangutan

Orangutans have the reddest hair around. Ophelia's was especially vibrant. It caught the sun's rays and sparkled. Her mother brushed it daily and everybody commented on her wonderful locks. Until one day, about four weeks before the rainy season, it started to fall out! Not in strands, but in huge bunches. Ophelia was beside herself with anguish. She cried and cried. Lost her appetite. She went into a shell and would not speak with anyone. Even her mom could not get her to talk. Despondent, Ophelia stayed home from forest school. While the other young orangutans were learning how to fend for themselves and survive in the forest, she wouldn't even go out. With patches of pink skin and long strands of red islands spotted around her body, she did look rather strange. It was hard for her mom to keep her spirits up. She and all her neighboring mom's had no explanation for the sudden disappearance of hair. They tried every remedy they could think of. Eucalyptus paste mixed with avocados. Lemon juice and cashew seed. Long blades of grass mixed in with red earth and spring water. Nothing worked. So she sent a message along the forest line, calling her brother Morty to come and help.

About 3 days later, Morty showed up. He had got the message, via macaws, spider monkeys and other animals who worked together to ensure animal communication was maintained, especially in times of personal emergency like this one. Although he had never seen such a happening as was befalling his niece, he suggested a novel idea. "Let's go to the ocean" he said. He had no idea what the ocean might bring, but the trip would give him time to think. And he would not take no for an answer. This was an instruction, not an offer. Since Ophelias's mother could use a break from the daily encouragement and the toll this took on her so she thankfully accepted Morty's suggestion. Off they went, Morty and Ophelia, just the two of them. Heading for the Indian Ocean. Of course Morty had been there many times before, but for Ophelia it was a new adventure. And he made her promise; "Ophelia, you must promise me that when we get there you will join me in swimming. You have to trust me that you will enjoy it. No matter what any other 'orangus' say or do, promise me you will go for a swim. Let's just go and have some fun!"

And so she promised. "OK Uncle Morty. I will go for a swim."

Morty had a feeling, that maybe the salt water might be good for her skin. Something new had to be tried. Ophelia's mother had exhausted all the other options that Morty could think of.

The journey covered many miles of forest and some open land. The two of them swung along, tree limb to tree limb. Gamboling along the grassy fields, climbing back into trees. Missing all that hair, she was quite comfortable in the late summer heat as long as the sections on grassy plains were not too long. There was no escaping the sun in the absence of trees. Ophelia's mother had cautioned her about spending too much time in the sun and made Uncle Morty promise he would not keep her on the beach to rest, but under shade of trees. So they journeyed on. Ophelia whistling merrily, every now and then cursing the blistering sun, but never out loud. She was well mannered, always respectful of adults and very much a proper female orangutan. (The males were another story, but that really is another story!) The trip did take her mind off her hair problem as she was enjoying new scenery. Fortunately they did not encounter any other large animals on the way. The occasional rodent would scamper away, mindful of the big creatures bearing down on them. And their objective was to stay clear of the big orangutans. Whether they had hair or not was a non issue for them. Anything large was a potential threat. Of course Morty and Ophelia laughed at this. The mere thought of eating the flesh of another creature was so ridiculous to them, that it was laughable.

When they got to the ocean, Morty paused at the break between forest and beach. He knew the spectacle of a wide open sea, stretching beyond one's vision, was an image to be forever imprinted onto a memory. He wanted Ophelia to always remember such new experiences. He was quiet for a moment, allowing Ophelia the pleasure of digesting this miracle without need of a conversation. And so they sat there, watching the waves wash gently on shore. The ocean was in between tides, so they had timed their arrival quite nicely. No massive surf to worry about and spoil the sensation of swimming in a salty basin. Morty had enjoyed swimming for many years, and was the ideal guide for a first timer like Ophelia.

"Well Ophelia, what do you think? Should we give it a whirl?"

"I don't know uncle Morty. It's so...big!" she replied. It was indeed big. But Ophelia also sensed that there was a marvelous beauty in that huge body of water. And with Uncle Morty next to her she felt safe.

"Come on girl" said Morty "Follow me and have a fun day!"

Uncle Morty had always been gentle and kind with Ophelia. And she had promised him that she would try. "OK Uncle Morty. You lead the way."

"Race you to the ocean!" he shouted and off he went, Ophelia jumping and running close behind. Morty ran and dove headfirst. Ophelia squealed with delight as she tripped and fell headlong into a coming wave. She jumped up, sputtering and coughing water, but laughing and laughing. And as she splashed her way in and out of the water she started to realize a wonderful thing. She enjoyed the feel of the water on her bare skin!

"Uncle Morty. This feels really good on my skin. It tingles and kind of makes me shiver. But in a good way."

"Ophelia I am so happy to hear that. Let's stay out for a while longer then." replied her uncle.

And so they did. The only living creatures for miles and miles. Just Morty and Ophelia having fun in the ocean. Morty would splash her and Ophelia would try to tackle her uncle, who playfully pretended to crash in a helpless heap whenever his niece tackled him.

"Uncle Morty. I'm so happy you brought me here. This is so much fun. And the water feels so good on my skin parts. It's so silky and smooth."

Morty beamed with satisfaction. "Ophelia honey, you just hang onto that feeling. When you are back home in the forest and things sometimes try to make you sad, you just remember that silky smooth feeling. And whenever you want to come back to the ocean you just put the word out to the forest line, and I'll come again. You're a special young lady, and even though you don't have full hair now, who's to say that won't change down the road? But one thing that you can control and keep forever, is that silky smooth feeling that makes you feel good all over. That is yours and hair or no hair, nobody can take that away from you."

Ophelia gave her uncle a big hug. "Thanks Uncle Morty. You're the best."

So even when you think the most terrible things are happening, you have the power to take from your positive experiences and over ride the bad feelings that are crowding your thoughts. Always remember your good times and use them to wash out the bad.

Polly the porcupine

The husky/lab cross, jumped from the boat as it touched the edge of the dock. The dog bounced along the boards and raced into the forest. Teisha's mouth was wide open, a huge grin expressing her joy as she started to explore this new space. Her human family had decided to build their summer home here, and who knew what treasures and surprises awaited her in the woods. Little did Teisha know that she would soon find a lifelong friend in this private island woodland.

Several hundred metres away, laying midway up a white spruce, its legs splayed over the branch like some Central American sloth, a northern porcupine snored contentedly in the mid day sun. This was Polly's favorite spot for her afternoon siesta. A wide shaft of August sunlight bathed her spiky fur, enveloping her in a toasty reverie. Every day, about this time, Polly would climb up this spruce tree and settle in for a snooze.

Polly followed a fairly mundane and regular pattern. She foraged for food in the morning, slept most of the afternoon, and went for long night walks, nibbling at blueberries and young flowers. Pine cones and bark formed the core of her diet during the day. She enjoyed this schedule and found no reason to change it. As the solitary porcupine on this island, and without any natural summer predators, it suited her fine. Mind you, winters were more problematic as coyotes and wolves and lynx would occasionally make their way over the frozen lake and explore food sources for their own existence. Polly had learned to spend most of her winters in the canopy, rarely making her way to the forest floor. She instinctively knew that larger animals represented a threat and were to be avoided. But summer provided opportunity to explore her domain and she did enjoy her morning and night expeditions. The island was quite large, at least from a mid size animal's perspective and one that moved quite slowly, so she took great delight in her wanderings.

As her mind was about to drift into contended sleep, she heard a quickly approaching rumble. "Now what on earth could that be?" she mused, opening one eye to see where from the commotion was coming. She vaguely made out a tan colored shape in the distance. "Couldn't possibly be a coyote" she thought. "Not at this time of year". Yet the rapidly approaching shape had the unmistakable look of a coyote, or even wolf. The animal had picked up her scent, and with its nose a mere inches above the grass and rocky landscape, it drew near to Polly's tree.

Teisha let out excited yelps and barks, not recognizing this new smell. "Whoo boy, I found something new to chase. Yahoo!" shouted out the dog, well within ear shot of Polly. Teisha was now at the base of the spruce tree and circled it madly, jumping up the trunk with her forepaws and barking away. Polly was now wide awake. And just a little miffed that this blonde creature had disturbed her nap. "What in God's name are you shouting for? I can hear you quite well you big lug!" she threw at Teisha. The dog however, could not see her and proceeded to jack up the volume of her yapping. "Oh for Lord's sake. How long do you plan on keeping up that racket? And where did you come from?" asked Polly. By this time she had raised herself up just a little, so the dog could see what it was directing it's excitement at.

"What are you?" asked Teisha, having never before encountered such a creature.

"I'm a porcupine you big dufus. What are you? You certainly don't look like a coyote, maybe a little but they don't wear jewelry. What is that around your neck?"

Teisha was equally surprised to see such a strange creature. Never before had she encountered a porcupine. Lucky for her!

"I'm Teisha. I'm a dog. What's a coyote? And what do you do? Do you eat rabbits?"

"No you silly thing. I'm a herbivore. Berries and nuts and flowers. Why? Do you eat rabbits?"

"Whenever I can catch them" Teisha replied. Which was unfortunately, at least for her that is, very few and far between. In fact, she had only managed to catch one rabbit in all her life! And even that one managed to escape because Teisha was so surprised at catching it, her jaw dropped for a moment and the rabbit made its getaway.

"Well" said Polly "You best go away then. If you eat meat, I don't think I want to get to know you. Know what I mean!"

"Ahh come on down" said Teisha. "Let's be friends"

"Yeah, right" laughed Polly "As if I'm going to trust what looks to me to be just another variation on coyote"

"What's a coyote? Tell me!" demanded Teisha, belying her ignorance of most things 'country'. She was after all a city dog that had only now been given freedom to roam this island.

"Tell you what" said Polly. "Come back tomorrow, only a little later so you don't disturb my nap and maybe I'll chat with you some more."

And with that, she settled back in to her branch to finish her nap. Try as Teisha would to cajole her into telling her more, Polly was soon fast asleep. So Teisha wandered off and made her way back to her human owners campsite.

The following morning, Teisha awoke with the sunrise and wandered back to the interior where she had first encountered Polly. But by this time Polly had moved to another high tree during her nightly foraging. Teisha picked up her scent and was soon at the base of a beautiful birch tree, resplendent in summer foliage, its white bark reflecting the morning sun. She spotted Polly on the lowest branch and shouted a "Good morning!"

Polly opened a sleepy eye, saw her morning visitor and let out a sigh. "Sheesh. I didn't mean to come by this early. Don't you ever sleep?"

"Sure I do, but the sun is up. Come show me around. I want to learn more about this great place."

"Now how do I know that you won't dig those gnarly white teeth into my hide and end my beautiful life?" Polly asked.

"I promise. Cross my heart" said Teisha.

"Yeah right!" laughed Polly. "As if I'm going to trust you after a few hours. What was your name again?"

"Teisha. And you are Polly. See, I even remembered your name"

"That's only because you want to brag about the taste of my skin when you yack with your coyote buddies" said Polly.

"I told you, I'm not a coyote. I'm a dog. I don't even know what a coyote is."

"OK. Here's how we're going to play this" said Polly. "There are enough overhanging branches here, so I'm going to climb from tree to tree and show you around. You follow on the ground. And if I decide by the end of the day that you're OK, I'll come down and we can get to maybe, and I mean maybe, be friends."

"Great" said Teisha. She really did not have an interest in eating Polly. Having grown up in the city her diet consisted mostly of dry kibble with the occasional table scrap tossed in. But Polly, having lived her life completely in the wild, was wary of this strange animal that so much mirrored the coyotes and wolves who threatened her every winter. And so they set off on a discovery pathway. Polly in the trees, moving as best she could from branch to branch and Teisha on the ground, learning more in one morning than she had in her entire lifetime of urban dwelling. Polly pointed out every new color. "That is a northern daisy; see how it is just opening its flowers to the morning sun. And over there is a little chipmunk. Leave it alone silly! If I'm going to trust you, then you have to show me you can live without eating any four legged creature you see!"

As the morning expanded, Teisha grew to appreciate the wonders of this island and Polly gradually lost her fear of this coyote like animal. So that by mid afternoon, Polly and Teisha were roaming around together on the ground, side by side, exchanging stories about their oh so different lives. Teisha trying to describe streetcars running on steel rails, and Polly attempting to articulate the brilliance of the northern lights. One thing they had in common? They both loved to chat! So by the afternoon, they were solidly on way to being best friends. For the rest of that week, until Teisha had to return to the city with her human owners, she and Polly would rendezvous daily.

Friendship can be had and shared between very different peoples and different things.

Quan the quetzal

The quetzal is arguably the most magnificent bird of all. Not to put down glorious birds like macaws and cockatoos, but the quetzal is truly special. It was highly prized in Aztec and Mayan culture. Only the high priests of Aztec religion and community chiefs could wear quetzal feathers. They wove it into their robes or headdress. The tail feathers were so valued, they were even used as currency. You can picture what a splendid sight it is, to see 3 feet of tail feathers swishing through the air. Never mind that the birds body is also a fabulous red with gold and green highlights. And quetzals are proud of the fact they look good. You can see it in the way they carry their heads high.

Quan the quetzal carried his head very high. He was in the prime of his life. Young. Single. And with superb health that made his feathers shine. When Quan flew, everybody took notice. He was such a special bird, that the Mayans had made it illegal to kill or capture Quan. Anybody caught breaking this law would be banished from the Mayan city. That was not a pleasant outcome, since banishment meant you had to survive in the jungle on your own. And with rumours aplenty about the coming of the Spanish conquistadors, one certainly did not want to get caught between two peoples, neither one of which would favour you as a friend.

Not only was Quan well known to the high Mayan priests, Quan also had lots of quetzal friends. Most of them were so absorbed with their good looks, that they flew with their heads down, admiring their tails and coloured feathers. Yes they were all very beautiful, but because of their narcissism, many never made it to a ripe old age. Their penchant for admiring themselves in flight made it easy to trap them in nets. They would be flying around, swooping and sweeping the sky, and then crash into nets the Mayans had set. And so end up in a head dress or part of somebody's robe! Or they would smash into a branch, scattering feathers as they struggled to regain their balance. Or an even more ignoble end would be to crash headfirst into a tree while admiring one's plumage, tumble to the ground and smack dab in front of a jungle predator like a jaguar! No need to describe what followed from that kind of a scenario!

Try as he might, Quan could not get his quetzal buddies to understand that flying with your head high and looking ahead and around you, was not just a safe way to fly, but also to appreciate the beauty of the surroundings. They all said he did not have to worry any way, because he had been designated a special quetzal. But that was besides the point. Quan understood that beauty was a God given gift, and it should be accepted but never flaunted.

One fine summer day, with the sun beaming down through the jungle canopy, Quan was enjoying a flight through the forest. He quite liked the way he was able to quickly change direction by maneuvering his tail back and forth. Swooshing between branches and massive tree trunks. Flying almost sideways thru tangles of vines, he barely brushed them as he cruised around. Quan delighted in flight, not in the image of flight. He was a true flyer. He looked ahead, he looked around and only occasionally did he look down. And looking ahead is when he spotted something that did not belong in the jungle. He could see it from miles away, even thru the tangle of vines and branches. Something was reflecting the sunlight in a very unnatural way. Quan knew what sunlight reflecting on wet leaves looked light. Or rays that bounced off some shiny stones on the jungle floor. Or light gleaming on a river surface. The shining light he saw on that fateful day, was different somehow. It pierced the jungle canopy like a laser. It so blinded him that he grabbed a solid branch and stopped his flight to determine what the source and meaning of that brilliant light was. As he squinted his eyes and focused on the distant beams, his ears began to pick up another unusual and strange sound. Human voices! But not a melodious sound like Mayan. No. This was a strange language. Angry. It was yelling and shouting. Coarse. The sound of men who were alien to life in the jungle. And then he saw them. Spanish soldiers clad in steel and bronze armour! The rumours were true. Conquistadors!

Of course he did not understand this at the time, but soldiers they were. And stumbling and hacking their way thru the thick mass of understory heading for the Mayan city! Quan sensed that these men were not traders like so many others who came and went thru the jungle. There were too many to be simply traders. He estimated at least 300. And from their angry voices and shiny armour, they looked very much like raiders from other Mayan cities. He had heard the stories from his father and his father before him. These humans were coming to steal and destroy. He knew what he had to do.

Quan leaped from the branch and headed back to the city. His flight from the city had taken him almost an hour that morning so his guess was the raiders would not be arriving until much later in the night, perhaps 8 hours later. Still, there was no time to waste. And he swooshed and swished his way back with haste. He flew directly to the main temple and circled the peak until he spotted the head priest. The priest recognized Quan and beckoned him to come near. Quan screeched in a voice that was full of terror.

"They are here. They are coming. The raiders are near!"

"Who is near?" asked the high priest. "What do you mean the raiders?"

"The men with shiny armour and long spears. They speak a strange language, full of hate and anger." replied Quan. "They will be upon the city by nightfall, they come from the east."

"Did you see them with your own eyes?"

"Of course. I flew straight to the temple as fast as I could."

"So it has been foretold" said the priest. "We must now make quick preparations to leave. Go and tell your families and spread the word. We will be leaving by the west gate and head south to the old city. I will strike the alarm so all can gather their possessions and flee. None can be left behind. Thank you Quan. Your strength and your beauty are without equal. We will gather together again when we reach the old city and mark a special celebration for you and all quetzals. Our saviour bird."

And so it was that the entire city was mobilized and organized. Preparations had been made well in advance so it was now just a matter of everybody doing their part. A stream of humanity headed for the western gate. Pulling carts and carrying loaded baskets. They left their beloved city behind, knowing that it was very unlikely they would ever be back. Likewise the quetzals and other forest birds and animals all headed south as well. For how long nobody knew, but at least for now Quan had saved the Mayans. And saved his own kin too.

Keep your head up and eyes on the horizon. Like Quan the quetzal. He looked ahead, he looked around and only occasionally did he look down.

Rebecca the raven

The raven is the mythic bird of Haida culture, Haidas being one of Canada's first nations indigenous peoples. Legend has it that ravens were present at the beginning of the world. The Haida believe the raven is responsible for human creation. Legend has it that raven spotted some creatures trapped in a clam. He introduced them to another set of creatures, similarly gathered in a mollusk, thus setting the 'stage' for the male and female of the human species. This ability to influence (as well as to mimic sounds) got raven the reputation of trickster. For many of the indigenous peoples, the raven is a powerful totem, both protector and spirit guide. He's a shape-shifter, messenger and a symbol of transformation. Haida culture and history also says the raven brought Sun to mankind. Raven myths hold this bird to be of high intelligence and to have a profound concern for humans. In fact, it is even believed the raven has healing powers. In a nutshell, this is one mighty powerful and influential bird.

Rebecca, the central figure in our story, was born into a family of ravens that had developed their trickster capabilities to such a high degree, they even held classes for other ravens who wished to learn more of the so-called dark arts. As she got older and her trickster and shape shifting powers grew, Rebecca's raven clan assigned her a new role as teacher. Up until now, her time had been spent refining her talents and tricking her clan whenever the occasion or mood suited her. On one occasion she had shifted herself to look like a carved raven and inserted her shifted shape onto a totem pole. Rebecca sat on the shore by the Haida long house as humans came and went, oblivious to the fact the carving on the totem pole was a shape shifter raven. Except for the very old and wise ravens in her clan, none of her friends knew either. They would land on the carved wings, and when least expected Rebecca would shift back into raven form causing her friends to tumble to the ground. She thought it quite humorous but her friends took exception to the bruises they suffered because of her trick. They warned her that one day her tricks would get her into serious trouble. Rebecca did not have many close friends in her clan.

So when the word got out, that Rebecca would be one of the new teachers, her clan peers were quite dumbfounded. That a major trickster would be assigned such a prestigious role was unusual to say the least. But it made sense. She was one of the best shape shifters. What she needed to learn was the application of those talents to occasionally helping others. Clan elders encouraged her to think of ways she could use her brilliant skill to help her community, and the human community which viewed ravens as almost God like creatures.

"Don't waste your energies and talents on hijinks" cautioned an old master. "There is a limit to what the great spirit will tolerate, even for someone as talented as you. The great spirit did not endow you with this marvellous energy for you to play tricks on your friends. We all need to laugh, but when laughter is all you know, then how will you recognize trouble and tragedy? Those will be times when your tricks could be used to do good, maybe even save lives. You think about that."

Rebecca thought about it.   She thought about it enough to keep her lessons in the classroom focused so her new students did learn some of her tricks and skills. Being in a classroom setting at least forced her to be disciplined and organize her trickster abilities. That was something she had not before done, actually practising the same skill set over and over until it became second nature.   Instead of commiting herself only to fun, she was making a commitment to helping others. In a way, the elders were achieving their objectives with Rebecca, forcing her to do good in the community.

But, as soon as her classes ended, Rebecca would soar into the sky, looking for targets to have some fun with. Or if there was nobody around to trick, then she would just turn herself into a rock or tree and observe the goings on.

On this day, Rebecca's fun hunt took her out over the open water of the Pacific. She had spotted a flock of eagles heading out over open water and thought that was unusual. Rebecca had tried on several occasions to shift her shape into an eagle, but she had so far been unable to assume an eagle's shape. It would be years before she could acquire the skill to shift into another live animal shape. Totem poles and rocks and even trees were one thing. But even a trickster with Rebecca's skill set would need years of discipline and practice before the great spirit would allow a shift into another body. Eagles would likely remain off limits to shape shifters, so revered were they.

Eagles won't normally fly over too much open water, but these guys were definitely heading out to sea. Being the inquisitive raven she was, off she went after them. She tried to keep pace as they went soaring on the thermal currents, circling ever higher. The eagles were going further and further over the ocean. They were probably looking for salmon that were coming back to mainland to lay their eggs. That would be the only thing that could explain their flight path so far over water. Try as she might, Rebecca could not keep pace. They soon left her soaring on her own as they faded far away. Rebeccas was so far out over the ocean, that land was barely visible behind her.

She had enough sense to recognize that any further flying would become problematic, in posing difficulty returning to shore. So she turned around and began heading back. That is when she spotted a fishing boat to the north. Thinking it might be a good idea to head there and land on the boat for a little rest, she started a downward glide toward the boat. As she got nearer, it struck her that something was not quite right. Rebecca could not determine exactly what it was, but something about the boat looked odd. And then it hit her. The boat was upside down! And floundering in the water were several orange shapes. People! There were four fishermen in the water, and no lifeboat to be seen. One of them looked like he was trying to get up on the upturned hull, but it was too slippery and too high a vertical wall to climb. And so Rebecca swung into action. It was like a voice in her head commanded her to do some good. She plunged downward as fast as she could go.

When she hit the water, she shape shifted into a redwood log. With lots of bark. The fishermen saw the log and all four swam to it, climbing on top and hanging onto the bark. And so they bobbed up and down with the sea, only now they had something to hang onto.

About thirty minutes later, a rescue helicopter could be seen heading for the sailors. They had managed to place a Mayday call just before their fishing boat overturned. It took that long for the chopper crew to scramble, leave their base and make it to the boat. As the chopper got within visual range of the boat, the fishing crew raised their arms, and the chopper dropped a lifeboat into the ocean. As soon as it hit the water, it inflated. The men were all able to swim to it and climb aboard. By the time they all climbed aboard and looked back to where they had left the log, Rebecca had shifted back to raven shape and was caw cawing with pleasure as she propelled herself back into the sky and towards home. Try as they might, the fishermen could not locate that redwood log, but they all swore after, that there had been one, and its presence saved their lives. For without that half hour when they hung onto the log, they likely would have persihed in the cold Pacific water.

The helicopter crew also looked for the log, but found no sight of it. Everybody concluded afterwards that it likely was waterlogged and simply slipped under the water surface. But Rebecca knew better, and she recounted this story to the clan. Some of the elders doubted it, but when they saw the helicopter flying back to shore, and shortly after, a bright red inflatable lifeboat landing on the beach by the totem poles, everybody had to accept that Rebecca had indeed shape shifted and saved their lives. Rebecca's adventure on the Pacific became known to the clan as "the Redwood log story" and it was told to all ravens for generations after Rebecca had died and gone to join the great spirit.

Sometimes it is good to change direction and do something completely different.

Soriana the swan

Soriana was a glorious trumpet swan. She loved to strech her neck skwyard and let out blasts of sound that made anything in the vicinity take note. Her mate Abu, another white beauty, would scold her for drawing so much attention to them.

"One of these days your trumpeting is going to get us into trouble. It's not enough that we're already standing out with our brilliant white feathers. You need to sing so loud that it almost hurts the ears."

"Oh don't be silly" she laughed "It's what we do. We're trumpet swans."

Indeed they were trumpet swans, but Abu did have a good point. Their home was a section of river that flowed thru the center of Consecon. Consecon was a small town, maybe only 500 humans, but it was still a town. So far the local people had not minded the swans in their midst. In fact, the vast majority quite liked the fact they could enjoy the beauty of these large birds so close to their homes. The people in the community would make sure the swans always had corn to eat. And of course tourists would also feed the birds, although this practice was not encouraged since gummy bears are not really a good source of vitamins for anybody, let alone these beautiful birds!

The loud trumpeting was just something they put up with. And it was not as if Soriana stretched her vocal cords in the dead of night when people were trying to sleep. She mostly sang in daytime. She delighted in honking loudly whenever someone tossed a very special treat to them. Sunflower seeds, unsalted, were a particular source of joy to both the birds. Her mate would even let out a brief honk to express his thanks when a few sunflower seeds were offered.

Just at the end of their stretch of river, an old mill had been converted to a pub. And a small deck looked out onto the Mill Pond as it was called. Locals and the occasional tourist would sit out there on bright summer days, quaffing pints of cold beer and munching on bar food. The owner of the Mill Pub had a thing about lighting candles, and he often would have several burning. It did look very pretty at night, but the owner would too often forget where he had lit the candles. His staff inevitably had to make sure they were all found and blown out before they locked up for the night.

But on this particular night, they missed one candle. It had been lit behind a large potted plant, and with the evening sun shining in, the glow just melded in with the suns rays. The last of the staff went out and locked up. And the candle kept burning. And burning. It was a very large candle so it took some time to burn down. But by night time, it was dripping wax onto the floor. The floor was the original wood mill floor. Very dry. And the flame caught the line of wax and shot down to the floor.

This was all happening very late at night, with the townspeople already fast asleep in their houses. Even the swans were just silently gliding around the pond, stretching their legs before they too would retire for the night. As they swept past the deck of the Mill Pond, Soriana said to her mate:

"Do you see that bright glow in there? It just does not look normal."

And she was right. The puddle of wax was now a small pool of flames. Very quickly the flames were spreading along the floor, first along the wax pool and then as the heat and amount of flames increased, it started to lap at the wood walls.

"Oh Lordy" said her mate "I do believe the Mill Pub is burning"

And that is when Soriana started to honk and sing as loud as she could. In a matter of a few seconds, several townsfolk who lived nearby were out on the street in their pyjamas to see what Soriana was fussing about. And they saw immediately. By this time smoke was starting to pour out the river side windows of the pub. The townsfolk swung into action. Grabbing pails of water and running to the Mill Pub. With an axe they broke the front door down and rushed in, tossing water as they went. In a matter of a minute, there was a fire line going to the river and buckets passed back and forth. Throughout this fire rescue, Soriana and even her mate, honked with abandon. It was like a shot of adrenalin to the fire crew. They worked furiously. And they succeeded in putting out the fire!

There was some damage, but with a solid airing out and some sanding of the wood that had burned, within a few days the pub re-opened. Crowds packed the place for weeks thereafter for the people had gained a real appreciation for the historic beauty of the building. They seemed to have a new found appreciation for this landmark gem which they had till now taken for granted. And the swans? Well, Soriana became legend. The town council even voted to make her the representative brand or logo on all their letterhead and literature. Soriana's picture was carved into the wooden sign at the town limits and underneath the population number was a sentence that read:

"Home of the legendary swan Soriana!"

So remember, sometimes you have to yell to be heard.

Tony the tarantula

Tarantulas are not the most attractive of critters, in fact they probably define what we think of as creepy. And Tony was about the creepiest of tarantulas imaginable. He had hairs growing out of his hair. He had bumps and nodules jutting out of his legs. And don't forget, tarantulas have 8 legs so that's a lot of bumps and nodules! It was very hard for Tony to play with other critters. He'd been trying to play with bigger critters and almost got squashed many times had it not been for his lighting quick speed in getting away. And his looks, most unpleasant by usual standards of what is and is not beautiful, turned away many opportunities for play. Other kids just did not want to play with Tony. They called him hurtful names. They taunted him. They laughed at him. Growing up as a tarantula was a difficult thing. Growing up as a creepy tarantula was doubly hard on a kid. Tony was having a very hard time enjoying his youth.

One day, as he was skipping along (yes tarantulas do skip, takes amazing hand/eye coordination let me tell you) Tony saw what he at first thought must be some colourful waste paper thrown away by humans. As he approached the red and yellow and purple coloured ball , he realized that it was in fact another spider! A very colourful and different spider. Tony jumped up to the spider and caused the other spider to tumble over backwards in fright. "What do you think you are doing?" shouted the other spider. "You scared the living daylights right out of me! Do you want me to have a heart attack?"

Tony laughed and replied: "Hey, I'm sorry. I was just so excited to see another spider so different." The coloured spider shot back "And what is that supposed to mean? Do you think I'm funny?" To which Tony replied "Well tell me a joke and we'll see if I laugh.'" That made the other spider giggle. "My name is Octavio. What's yours?"

"Tony. I'm Tony the tarantula."

"Whoo, is that supposed to scare me away, I'm shivering with fright!"

"Well, if you really want to shake I can give you a quick shot of poison and you'll be shaking like a leaf."

They bantered back and forth for a few minutes, trading friendly insults and boasting about their prowess. Octavio and Tony quickly warmed to each other and before they knew it they were sauntering along together. "So tell me Octavio, do you have any buddies you hang out with?" to which Octavio replied "No, it's really hard getting playmates when you scare people away. How about you?" Tony responded "Yeah, I know exactly what you mean. Every time, well almost every time. I try to join a group in any game they all shoot back with really mean things about how I look, and how different I am. I'm trying to be nice but it's getting harder and harder. And then there are the guys who say they will play but spend the whole time trying to squash you. It's getting very frustrating."

"Hey" said Octavio "How about if you and I hang out together? I like you and I bet you're a pretty good soccer player." Tony said "Well, I do like the game but every time I've played I spend all my time looking out that i don't get squashed. So it's never any fun with the other guys. Let's get a ball from my place and kick it around."

Octavio said "That's a great idea! Let's go." And so off they went to Tony's to get a ball. Both spiders were quite adept at dribbling and passing the ball back and forth. They delighted in trying to outdo each other with fancy multi-legged moves. A dribble off one to the other, a bounce to the third, a kick to the fourth, a soft lob to the fifth and on and on. They hooted and hollered with laughter at each progressively complicated move. "Wow man, you are good" said Tony. To which Octavio also complimented "No man, you are good."

Their play had taken them close to the soccer pitch where a group of other kids were kicking a ball back and forth as well. They all stopped to watch in amazement as Tony and Octavio handled the ball like a couple of semi-pro players. Their jaws dropped as they realized one by one, that one of the spiders was the same kid Tony, whom they had been mocking and taunting. None of them opened their mouths to speak; they did not know what to say. Tony then saw where he and Octavio had ended up and stopped his play, one foot balanced on top of the soccer ball. Tony spoke. "Hi guys. This is my new friend Octavio." They all nodded in Octavio's direction and started an avalanche of praise. "Wow, you guys are good. That is incredible. Show me how you did that double pop move."

And as their praise and accompanying slaps on the back continued, Tony and Octavio did not say a word. They reveled in the positive words that were floating around them. Both realized that an apology for past misbehaviour was no longer necessary. The acceptance and praise of their old tormentors was quickly eliminating the bad feelings that had tainted their relationship with these other kids.

Tony and Octavio had shown the other kids that it's not what's outside that counts. It's what you do and how you do it. Do whatever you do, but do it well and do it without hurting anybody else.

Ukuru the Ulysses butterfly

Ulysses or Blue Morph butterflies are arguably the most beautiful butterflies in the world. Their iridescent blue wings capture sunlight and shimmer like mirrored disco balls. They can be found in Central America, and love to taste nectar from gigantic blossoms of the hibiscus flower.

Ukuru was a glorious specimen of blue Morph. His wingspan measured 15cm tip to tip. And his flight pattern was a very jagged series of cuts. Just about all butterflies have a strange flight pattern, going up and down and changing direction quite suddenly. When you watch butterflies in the air, it almost seems like they are a bit tipsy. Who knows, maybe that is why they love to drink nectar so much! In the hot sun it might start to ferment, just like fruit does. For you young kids, that means it starts to produce alcohol and too much of that makes your balance go topsy turvy. (Ask your mom or dad.)

Ukuru could almost reverse direction 180 deg in mid flight. He had worked at that particular skill, the super quick change of direction. Now his long wingspan did give him an advantage, but he also just purely enjoyed flight. Ukuru loved to fly. And, he could fly upside down. That is a really difficult trick and not too many butterflies can do it. But Ukuru had mastered it. With enough dry leaves on the ground, and leaves falling all the time in the jungle, Ukuru just vanished and became a part of nature when he flew upside down. The underside of a Ulysses' wing looks like the face of a big brown insect with huge black eyes. This was one of nature's defense tools that had been given to the Ulysses. That way, if they were under attack, say from a large bird, they could fold up their wings and almost disappear into the shrubbery. And the large black dot made most predators think twice about an attack, because it made it look as if there was a big animal somewhere behind.

Ukuru had developed this skill out of the sheer pleasure he got from flying. He wanted to take his natural abilities and refine them to a level that was beyond his butterfly buddies. They all looked absolutely beautiful, but very few of them took the time or energy to learn new skills. But if they happened to be in mid air when a toucan or parrot spotted them, it was very hard to disappear because of those magnificent blue wings. The opportunity to put this maneuver into play, other than for fun, had not yet presented itself. Up until today.

Ukuru had been tasting hibiscus nectar from a group of shrubs by the side of a clearing. These plants received lots of direct sunlight, so their blossoms were huge and the resulting nectar was very sweet. As he flitted from flower to flower, Ukuru was unaware of an eagle that was circling high above the tree tops. The eagle was watching Ukuru's flight from flower to flower, planning his dive. And when Ukuru jumped off a bold red flower and started his jagged flight across the clearing to the flowers tempting him from the other side, the eagle began his dive bomb attack. According to the eagle's calculations, he would hit Ukuru almost dead centre in the middle of the clearing. And by the size of this blue morph he would soon be tasting a delicious snack.

Down, down he rocketed. And Ukuru's flight path zigged and zagged. It was seconds to impact. And then by a stroke of luck, Ukuru flipped upside down. Just for fun. But that decision would save his life. For he saw the eagle bearing down on him. He kept zigging and zagging, but now upside down. And the eagle lost sight of those iridescent blue wings. Ukuru had disappeared amongst the falling brown leaves, looking to the eagle like just another of the hundreds of leaves zigging and zagging to the jungle floor. It was just long enough for Ukuru to zig and zag over to the side of the clearing where he once again could fly right side up, only this time under the shrubs. The eagle pulled up and reversed direction going back up into the sky, slightly confused as to how he could have lost sight of that blazing blue meal.

Ukuru had dodged a bullet. And the speed with which eagles could dive, made them almost as fast as bullets. That skill of flying upside down had saved his life.

Don't rely on good looks alone. You need skills to prosper.

Victor the vulture

Victor the vulture had it made. He lived on a large island called Prince Edward County. This island jutted out into Lake Ontario. Victor and his family could feast on deer that had been killed by wolves and coyotes, on raccoons and skunks and rabbits that were hit by cars. I know it is not a pretty sight to imagine, but such is the life of vultures. They scavenge and they clean up the mess. Kind of like nature's janitors. They are not pretty birds. But then, considering what their function is, I can't imagine a pretty bird like a white swan would be acting as nature's janitor. So we'll accept that this hard working bird won't win any beauty contests! And really, does it matter what it looks like as long as the mess gets cleaned up?

Victor and his buddies delighted in getting to a carcass (that's a fancy name for dead animal) before any other vultures. They would pick away at the tastiest bits (I won't describe what those are, kind of gross) and then take off in search of more snacks. This strategy of eating removed the strong odour from a carcass and made it difficult for other birds and animals to find the food. And that meant a lot of this food spoiled and became inedible for other birds and animals. Why was this a problem? Well. In winter time, when food supplies were scarce anyways, many other animals, especially coyotes and wolves who found it hard to hunt in deep snow, went hungry because they could not smell a carcass with the internals removed. Nobody would have paid much attention to this except one day Victor's mother and her friends came upon a snack that Victor and his buddies had just left. She knew it was Victor as she watched them fly away. Mom's know how their kids look and fly, even from far away. They just do. It's a peculiar thing that all mothers understand.

So when they landed and saw all the food that Victor and his friends had left, they were quite upset. "I cannot believe my eyes" said momma vulture. "Those boys could not have been here for longer than 5 minutes. This speed snacking has got to stop, especially since our coyote and wolf friends have been complaining about the shortage of deer in the County. And with winter coming they are worried about the survival of their pups." So momma vulture sprang up and beat her wings with a furious motion. She caught an updraft and took off after her son. By this time Victor and his buddies had disappeared over the horizon but momma had a good idea where they were going. The boys usually dropped out of the sky at Bakker Rd beach, a gorgeous strip of sandy beach which hardly anybody knew about.

Momma vulture saw the boys hanging out on a long piece of driftwood at the north end of the beach. She swooped down and surprised them all, alighting on the log. The boys cackled and squawked, taken completely by surprise.   Victor said "Hi momma. What brings you here?"

Momma responded "There is something i want you boys to see. Follow me." And with that she jumped back up, beating once again to reach gliding altitude. Victor and his buddies knew better than to disobey momma and they dutifully followed. It was a short flight back to the carcass. Momma was already sitting there, ripping away at the flesh.

"Hey momma. We knew this was here. We just finished eating a while ago but thanks for showing it to us anyway." said Victor, completely oblivious to why his mother had brought him back.

"You really think I brought you back here for a meal?" questioned his mother. "Try to put that teenage brain of yours into another gear and think about why I brought you here."

Victor squinted his eyes, his brain wrestling with the question. But try as he might, he just could not get near to the reason.

"I don't know momma. Maybe like you were worried about us not getting enough food?" he said

"You silly boys." replied momma. "I just told you I did not bring you back for a meal. I know you are old enough to scavenge for your own food now. I taught you how, remember!"

She continued tearing away at the carcass and watched out of the corner of her eye as the boys started to do the same. One by one they settled into the carcass, finding more and more tasty bits that they had previously ignored.

"Man, I didn't realize I was still so hungry'" said one of Victor's buddies. "We should have stayed here and feasted a little more."

"Bingo" shouted the momma vulture. "There is hope for you boys yet. Yes, you should have stayed here and eaten your fill. Because every time you nibble at just the tasty internals of a carcass and leave the rest, you deny our wolf and coyote brothers and sisters an opportunity to find the food. You guys can spot the meals from high up in the sky, but unless the coyotes and wolves can smell the food, the only way they will find it in winter is if they stumble right onto it. We owe it to those guys to make sure they can survive winter too. Don't forget they are the ones we also rely on when winter is really bad and snow covers almost everything. I remember winters when your father and I had only scraps of bone to munch on because the cold was so intense, hardly any little critters came out of their burrows. But we could see gatherings of our four footed friends and knew that if we waited long enough for them to leave, we could swoop in and clean up the remainder. So file this little lesson into a more readily accessible part of your brains. Everybody deserves the right to a decent meal. And if you are enjoying a superb meal, then make sure that a basic meal is leftover for others."

Donate waste food. There are still too many people going hungry.

Waldo the walrus

Waldo was slow, even for a walrus. He had always been a little slower, a little noisier and just a little back on the learning curve. As he grew bigger, those problems just seemed to get worse. He'd lumber through the water while his buddy walruses were easily gorging on sardines, darting in and out of the huge school. But Waldo had a problem gliding, he never got the hang of how to creep up on those sardines. You'd think that walruses, because of their huge size, would scare away any smaller bait fish, but walruses had developed a knack for gliding without moving their fins. Sure, they moved them to get to their targets, but when they were within 100 m of a potential dinner, they managed to shut down their appendages and just glide along, soundlessly getting closer and closer. Like a submerged log they would drift until the sardines were within reach. Then it was a series of gigantic gulps as they gorged on the silver fish. Not Waldo.

Whenever Waldo stopped moving his fins, he just dropped dead in the water and started to sink. Ever so slowly, but he would drop deeper and deeper. Of course he would have to move his fins a little to get himself going again. That movement would alert the sardines to impending danger. Off they went, and off went Waldo's supper. Over time, the other walruses started to avoid Waldo. Whenever he was a part of the dinner search, they rarely got enough sardines to even qualify as an appetizer, let alone a dinner. So one by one they found excuses to avoid fishing with Waldo. They were real nice about it, making up excuses that didn't attack Waldo's lack of fishing skills, but nevertheless Waldo felt he was a burden on the group. His mother did her best to bring sardines to him, but even that could not last forever. Waldo was already bigger than his momma. And she was gradually losing weight as she tried to take care of Waldo. Plus, she would soon be off to breed again, it's a natural thing. That meant Waldo would be left without any food at all. What to do?

Well Momma walrus knew that a radical change was required. She had done all she could. As a mother. As a caregiver. So she went on a long swim one morning, taking until much later in the afternoon to return. She did not tell anybody where she was going. Not even Waldo. This worried him to no end, when he looked for his mother that day. He knew her sacrifice was literally killing her, and she would have to leave soon. But he had thought she would at least tell him when it was time for her to go, and not just swim away without saying a word. So her return in the late afternoon was a huge relief to him.

"Momma. I was worried that you had left! For good."

"Oh silly boy, of course not. I would never leave without spending really good time with you. Come here, give me a hug."

"How come you were gone so long momma?" he asked.

Momma walrus looked at Waldo long and hard. And she beckoned him to come with her, as she swam a slight distance from the pod.

"Son, I'm going to tell you something now. And you cannot share this with anybody. Not until much later. Promise me."

Well, this was certainly a surprise to Waldo. Mysterious in a way. In fact it excited him to know that he would be the only one with his mother to know something so important. He knew his momma would not take him aside like that, and whisper secretly, unless it was indeed of huge importance.

"I'm sending you to meet somebody. A good friend from long ago. He's going to help you out and teach you some very important things. Especially about fishing"

" Who am I going to momma?"

"Bingo." replied his momma

"Bingo?" was all Waldo could respond, almost chuckling.

"Yes son, you will be mentored by my good friend Bingo. Don't laugh. Your father and I met Bingo many years ago. He was a guide for us during some very difficult times, before you were even born. He helped us to survive and I've asked Bingo to show you the same skills he taught to us."

Waldo was eager! "When do I go momma? I'm ready to learn. "

"I told Bingo we would come to meet him so if you are ready then let's go!"

Off they went. Momma in the lead, Waldo lumbering behind. His mother had a good fix on Waldo's rhythm so he did not feel rushed or pressured. They made good time and in a couple hours momma stopped at the base of a long shelf and said "This is where we shall meet Bingo."

They settled into some foraging and little games of touch and go with fish that came around. They ate their fill as the fish life was abundant around this shelf. Occasionally surfacing for air, both settled into a kind of walrus nap state, fins randomly moving to keep balance. They'd occasionally have to surface to get more air, Waldo more so than his Momma since he kept sinking, but most of the time they spent underwater enjoying the thermal springs that warmed the area around the shelf. Waldo headed for the surface.

"I'm going to nap on the rocks. Let me know when Bingo arrives."

"Momma walrus smiled and said "Oh you'll know when Bingo is here. Believe me you'll know."

Waldo had fallen completely asleep, snoring so loudly his mother heard him underwater.   She sensed a change in water pressure and thought "That's it, he's nearby."

Sure enough, a huge blue shadow showed itself, becoming larger and larger to the point it completely shut out the light coming from above. Bingo was here. A huge blue whale! Momma walrus greeted bingo with great enthusiasm and thanked him for coming thru.

"For you my pretty lady, I'd cross many oceans." replied Bingo. "So where is this young lad who needs some coaching?"

Momma walrus left Bingo and surfaced near the rock. "Honey, Bingo is here. Wake up and come underwater."

Waldo gave himself a good shake, and slipped back into the water. No sooner had he dove, when he came face to face with the biggest whale he had ever seen! And he shot back up to the top, catapulting himself back onto the rock.

"Momma there is huge whale right here. Aren't you scared?"

Momma walrus laughed and laughed. "Silly boy. That is Bingo. I didn't tell you he is a whale because I knew you'd be frightened. But fear not. Bingo is the best friend you could hope for. Come back underwater and meet him." Before he could slip back in, a geyser of water shot 20 ft into the air. "Oh honey, Bingo is giving you a show. Look at that."

Reluctantly Waldo slipped back into the water, and kept very close to his mother as they swam to Bingo's front, facing him. Bingo smiled and nodded at Waldo. "What's the matter big fella? Worried I was going to eat you?" And he let out a rolling laugh that echoed around the shelf and ridges underwater. "Relax. Just kidding! So you're the young hunter who needs some coaching?"

"Yes sir." was all Waldo could say, his body still shaking .

"Well Momma walrus, you've come a long way today so head on back to your pod. I'll take this young man under my wing and bring him back to you in a month's time. I think he'll be a new man." With that, Waldo gave his momma a big hug and joined Bingo on an adventure.

"Young man, I'm going to show you one thing that all large underwater creatures should learn. And it is this. Your mass is your weapon."

"But every time I try to catch fish, i keep scaring them away because I have trouble floating."

"Watch and learn" replied Bingo.

They soon came upon a school of sardines and krill. And to Waldo's amazement, instead of simply opening his mouth wide open, Bingo did a slow flip and came at the school vertically! He literally swam in sideways and just when the school of fish realized that this vertical blue post was a whale, Bingo flipped back to horizontal, opened his jaw and swallowed hundreds of fish!

"Try changing your body position too." said Bingo. All the small fish will be so totally unfamiliar with your shape, they will be momentarily spellbound. Instead of running away, they will curiously want to understand what is facing them. Is it threat or is it harmless. All creatures need to know. And by the time they realize you are in fact a walrus, it'll be too late for them.

"Will it work for me?" asked Waldo

"Let's keep swimming and look for more" replied Bingo. "And by the way, I'm OK with you going back to the surface to get some air. Don't forget, I can hold my breath way longer than you."

"Look up ahead' said Bingo. There is another school. Now remember what I said, just flip yourself so you come in vertical. And your flippers are pretty strong so you can keep that position longer than most of your buddies I'm sure."

Waldo did exactly that. He flipped vertical as Bingo stayed in the background. And sure enough, Waldo was able to get closer to a school of fish than he had ever got before! He flipped back to sideways, and just as they had done with Bingo, it was too late for the fish! Waldo charged right into them and was able to snag scores before they got away!

"Wow! This is awesome" he shouted "You've shown me a great tip. Thank you Bingo."

In the coming days, during their swim around, Bingo told Waldo some other fishing tips that Waldo was eager to try. Some worked for him and others, well, not so much. But that vertical flip that he learned on the first day would put him back on the road to getting stronger and accepted by his buddies in the pod.

Upon returning to his walrus pod, he was the biggest and strongest walrus. The bonus of being so healthy? Waldo had no trouble getting a mate! All he needed was somebody to show him a different way to fish. Bingo was that somebody.

We can learn from everybody, and everything. Never stop learning.

Xoxo the xenopus

Xoxo, pronounced HoHo, was a member of the xenopus family of frogs. The word is latin for "strange foot" and that is exactly what these creatures are. They have webbed feet which they use for fast propulsion through the water. The webbed feet also have quite the claws, and are used to rip apart all manner of food. These guys eat anything. It would not be unfair to describe them as underwater jackals. Xoxos are the cleanup crew. But sometimes even xenopuses don't want to clean up.

Cleanup was a concept that Xoxo was unfamiliar with. He left his things everywhere, and I do mean everywhere. Inside,outside, did not matter. It drove his schoolmates crazy. And since Xoxo and the fellow xenopuses lived at a boarding school there was no mother nor father to pick up his things. It fell to his classmates to always do the cleanup.

"I'm getting really tired of picking up after Xoxo." said one of the schoolboys. "I mean really, really tired. Why should we have to worry about Xoxo and his stuff?"

Murmurs of 'yes' and 'right on' filtered throughout the dormitory.

"It's not as if we don't have our own stuff to worry about." echoed another "Now we waste so much time looking out for Xoxo. And He's not even grateful! Never says thank you."

"Here's what I think we should do" said a third. "Let's start leaving our stuff on Xoxo's bunk! Not really important stuff, but things like socks, candy wrappers, empty cans, little stuff that will all together pile up to be big stuff! A pile of stuff on his bed."

Laughter resounded in the dormitory. All thought this was a grand idea. That would show Xoxo they were fed up.

"What if he just shoves it to the side?" asked one.

"Then we will just pile it back up on his bed when he's not looking. If we all work this together he won't be able to ignore it forever."

And so began the 'Xoxo project' as the boys came to call it. None expected this would drag on forever. At most, they thought a few days and Xoxo would finally understand. I mean, how much junk can anybody tolerate before it makes it hard to move around? Apparently Xoxo could tolerate a whole pile! On the first day, they had piled up a one foot high hill of socks, cans, paper, cardboard, t shirts and all sort of material. Nothing wet or sticky. Just stuff that a normal person would see and figure out there must be a message. Not Xoxo.

When he came in from outside, after the evening snack, and got ready for bed he simply took his arm and brushed all the stuff onto the floor! So the small mountain of stuff ended up on the floor. It did not seem to bother him any. The other boys tried to embarrass him but to no avail. He fell asleep in no time and the other xenopuses eventually fell asleep too, muttering curses.

The next morning, after Xoxo had dressed and left for class, a couple of the other xenopuses gathered up the stuff Xoxo had swept to the floor, and deposited it all back on his bed. And added a few other items. But that night, just like the first night, Xoxo simply brushed it all to the side again.

This back and forth game lasted well into the weekend. But the turning point came when there was so much stuff on Xoxo's bed, he could not sweep it all to the floor. Some was left on his bed. The pile had grown so much in 5 days that even Xoxo had to take notice.

"OK you guys. What's going on with all the garbage on my bed?" he asked.

Well, the dumbfounded looks and comments from his classmates just emphasized that Xoxo was clueless about his bad habit of leaving things everywhere.

"Are you dense or are you kidding us?" asked one.

"What do you mean dense? That sounds like an insult!" he replied

"Xoxo, can you really be so out of it?" asked another

"What do you mean, out of it?"

"Oh man, do you think we're doing this just for fun? We're trying to make a point you big dullard! You leave your stuff all over the place, and we have to pick up after you. All the time! It's not like it happens now and then. Every day you are dropping stuff. And then forgetting it, or ignoring it and moving on to something else. So we're trying to show you what it feels like."

There was a silence in the room for several moments. Xoxo did not speak. Nobody else spoke. Until finally Xoxo said "So why didn't you just say so. I never realized I was so bad. I promise I will pick up after myself with a little more care. "

And that is what it took for Xoxo to recognize his actions were making enemies of his classmates. Sometimes you have to almost rub someone's nose in the dirt before they see the light. We're all very busy with our lives, but it is so important to pick up your stuff. And put it back in a proper place. It will save you time looking for it. It will save your friendships. And your mother and father will respect you for it and maybe even let you borrow the car keys more often!

Clean up after yourself. Don't leave a mess for others.

Yangtze the yak

The yak is similar in appearance, although a bit smaller than the American bison. Both have long hair to withstand colder climates; the bison needs to survive North American winters and the yak in central Asian mountains. Yaks make excellent pack animals and are valuable for the roaming tribes of central Asia. These peoples follow their herds from summer to winter feeding grounds while carrying all their worldly possessions with. But they have also trained their yaks to do something else. Yak polo. I kid you not. You're all familiar with the game of polo right? Polo is a game where two teams of riders try to smack a hard ball using a wooden mallet very similar to a croquet mallet thru a set of goalposts. All this while riding a hairy yak just like they would a horse. Which brings us to our story about Yangtze.

Yangtze was born with only three legs. Nobody knows how this happened, but mother nature must have had some plans for Yangtze. His right foreleg only extended to just below the knee cap. As a young yak, he had learned to kind of hobble along on three legs, with the right foreleg just dangling in the breeze. So his other three legs became quite strong as did his three shoulders. Since he was quite a chatty companion to the other yaks, his master decided to keep him. It would have been easier to turn him into yak steak, but his presence always seemed to lighten up the other yaks, and they never complained about the packs and parcels they carried. It just did not seem right to complain when your buddy yak had to hobble his way thru life minus one leg. But as he matured, Yangtze got sadder and sadder as he had to stand on the sidelines and watch his fellow yaks engage in the game of yak polo. They would all bustle and run around the yak field carrying their masters and having a blast. Poor Yangtze could only cheer from the sidelines. He wanted to play. But with the missing leg, and not able to carry his master, the prospect of ever having fun in a yak polo game got dimmer and dimmer. And Yangtze got sadder and sadder. This troubled his master greatly, for he understood and appreciated how much Yangtze meant to the rest of the yaks. And the other masters also knew their yaks carried heavier loads for longer distances because of the ability of the good natured Yangtze to lighten their loads with his happy banter. But that banter was disappearing, gradually shifted aside by a melancholy yak who could not join his friends in a game of yak polo. The sadder Yangtze got, the slower the other yaks walked, and the less load they were able to carry. Yangtze did not understand this, but his happiness was an important contributor to the community's success. So when he was not happy, the community was not happy.

Now one of the masters, an older gentleman named Wai Chu, had lost a leg many years ago when he fell down a mountain side and suffered a terrible leg fracture. The fracture never healed properly, and Wai Chu ended up losing his leg. He was a resourceful man, and carved a wooden leg from a piece of uburu tree. He simply strapped on the wooden leg piece so he could continue walking with his buddies. If you did not know it, you'd never have guessed he had a wooden leg. Wai Chu had an idea.

He went to the nearby forest and looked around for the perfect piece of wood. He was going to carve a wooden leg for Yangtze! Yes. A replacement leg for a yak. Unheard of. But Wai Chu figured why not? It worked for him, so why not a yak. Nothing venture nothing gained as the old expression goes. If Yangtze continued on the present path of sadness, who knows what might befall the tribe.

Wai Chu spent the better part of that morning looking all thru the forest. And by noon he had found it. A beautiful dry length of uburu. He'd have to carve it some to the shape of a yak's leg, but it already had a little hollow on top that would fit almost perfectly into Yangtze's right foreleg. Just a wee bit of carving and modification. And so he brought it back to his yurt (those are the tent shelters that people in these parts use as their homes). He brought out his favourite carving tools and got to work. Wai Chu carved for the rest of that day. And by nightfall he had a beautifully fashioned yak leg ready for installation. But by then he was very tired and lay down for a good nap.

Next morning, bright and early, he awoke Yangtze's master.

"Come have a morning tea with me and I will show you a surprise"

Now the master was still a little sleepy, but surprises were usually good news. And he was in desperate need of some good news. He understood the other masters concerns about Yangtze and the impact the yak's sadness was having on everybody. So off he went with Wai Chu.

Wai Chu opened the flap of his yurt and they both stepped inside. Two mugs of steaming Chaga tea were on the round table along with some freshly baked quinoa cakes. They sat on the surrounding carpets and sipped and munched in silence. That was the tribal way, to first enjoy your food, and then engage in conversation. A few minutes passed before Wai Chu spoke.

"So tell me, my good friend. How is your young yak Yangtze doing these days?"

Yangtze's master knew full well that everybody understood the predicament so there was no purpose in hiding the truth.

"Yangtze is not happy Wai Chu. This you already know. I worry about him and what might become of all of us if things do not get better for my yak. But I just do not know what to do."

Wai Chu smiled. "Come with me to behind my yurt and I will show you something."

They got up from their breakfast tea, and the master followed Wai Chu out the door. They stepped around the back of the tent and the master's eyes almost fell from his head. There in front of him, stood Yangtze, but with four legs! The master blinked and shook his head, as if to shake away a dream that had somehow burned into his eyes. But there he stood. Yangtze with four legs. It was not until he stooped down to investigate that the master understood. What looked like a normal leg from afar, was really a sturdy piece of uburu wood that had been wrapped in yak fur! Not only that, but there was a saddle on Yangtze!

"I'd say go ahead, jump aboard" laughed Wai Chu "But I think it may yet be a little training is needed before your yak can accept a rider"

"I can't believe my eyes" responded the master. "This is incredible"

But true it was. Yangtze had a new leg. And in the coming weeks, he very quickly learned to accept his master on his back. And before the winter snows came, Yangtze was even able to participate in the games of yak polo. In fact, at times when the master could not reach the ball with his mallet, Yangtze was able to swing his wooden leg and strike the ball with such force and precision, he became known wide and far as Yangtze the Polo Yak! The other yaks once again shouldered heavy loads on their backs and in tribute to Yangtze, he was allowed to do the migrations without carrying anything. He sometimes did, just to prove to himself that he could, but his happy presence was worth more to the herd and the tribe than any ability to carry a load. Yangtze was back, better than ever.

So don't ever think your disability should bar you from trying new things or should make you sad. You can turn a disability into an ability.

Zoe the zebu

Zebus are little known mammals that can thrive in very hot climates. They are a form of cow and have a hump back. Zebus are very small animals and Zoe was particularly tiny, even for a Zebu. Normal Zebus are about a meter high but Zoe was just a tad over 50cm high. There were lots of dogs in Zoe's neighbourhood in Central Africa that were bigger than she. Most of the dogs enjoyed her company since she posed no threat, even though she did have the long zebu horns on her head. But she had not yet learned how to use them as a tool to defend herself against the roving bands of hyenas and lions that roamed the savannah as well. In fact, she found them to be quite a nuisance when playing with her friends. She had trouble making quick turns, thinking that the horns had a kind of will of their own, pulling her neck backwards. Often when grazing on the savannah she would catch the tips on the ground and stumble awkwardly. Her mom called it `growing pains` but Zoe the Zebu just never got the hang of it. The older she got, and the more her fellow Zebus joked about her stumbles, the less time she spent with the herd, preferring instead the company of the dogs and even smaller animals like groundhogs. Her mother started worrying that maybe Zoe`s stumbles were not simple growing pains, but a symptom of some kind of balance problem. And, she was worried that Zoe was not learning anything about being a Zebu, having spent most of her time with non Zebu critters. So she called the head Zebu over to have a chat with Zoe.

"So Zoe" he started. "How are things going?"

Zoe knew that was a loaded question. "How are things going?" What could he mean by that? As far as she was concerned "things" were going just fine. Except for the fact she stumbled a little and had trouble keeping up with the herd, she did not see any problem. So she responded.

"Things are just fine, thank you very much"

But the head zebu would not be satisfied with that. He knew Zoe's mom would not have called unless there was a concern.

"Really Zoe? Are you enjoying your time with the herd?"

Now that made Zoe think. She had not been spending much time with the herd. Most of her time was with the dogs and other smaller animals that hung around the herd. She had not given that much thought until this moment.

"Well actually sir" she said, "I've not been spending much time with the herd. I'm having fun with the dogs and other animals. Is something wrong?"

"No, no" replied head zebu. "Nothing is wrong. Your mother was just a bit concerned about you."

Zoe thought for a moment, "Now why would Mom be concerned?" She could not quite put a finger on the reason.

"Your Mom mentioned that you were having some balance issues" continued the head zebu. "I was wondering if it was bothering you any?"

So that's it thought Zoe. They have all been watching me and laughing at me. "I've been making a right regular fool of myself haven't I" she said as her Zebu face reddened considerably.

"No Zoe. Not at all. But I'm wondering if maybe I could be of some assistance to show you a few things?" Like all young Zebus, Zoe could not imagine what this old Zebu could possibly show her or teach her.

"Come with me and let me show you something". And off they went to the edges of the savannah where the brush started.

"See the grass here" said head zebu, pointing to the lush greenery under the shrubs. "Watch this." He started to graze at the edges and could only poke his huge head and massive horns a couple of feet into the shrubs before getting entangled. As he backed away he asked Zoe to try. So Zoe put her head down, stumbled a little, but was able to push her way into and under the shrubs, revealing ultra green grass that she joyfully nibbled at. Head Zebu called her, and she backed out from the shrubs, this time without stumbling at all.

"How did you do that?" asked head zebu with a sly grin on his face.

"Well, I just kind of pushed the shrubs out of the way and went in" said Zoe.

"But how come I cannot do that?" replied head zebu as he tried once again to bull his way in, this time getting a good sized scratch on his nose. "Ouch!" he exclaimed.

Zoe giggled, and went back in for another bite, carefully pushing the shrubs away, and even crouching down a little lower so she would get in without any scratch.

"Now tell me Zoe. Aside from maybe balancing your center of gravity a little more so you don't stumble, I think you have a big advantage over me. At least when it comes to finding the best grazing patches. The only way I can get at that grass under those shrubs, is to suffer a bunch of gashes and cuts. You on the other hand, being so low to the ground, can easily pop in and out of there and grab the best treats. Would you mind bringing me a bunch so I can enjoy those tasty munchies too?"

And so Zoe went back in, grabbed a serious mouthful of lush grasses and went to give them to head zebu. He gently took them and 'ooohd' and 'aaahhd' with delight. "Now Zoe, I'd like you to join the herd tomorrow as we come back to this spot. Promise me you will."

"I promise" she said. And the next day, Zoe bopped along with the herd, which quickly came to appreciate her ability to gather the tastiest grasses from hard to reach places, and accorded her a new respect. And the more time she spent with the herd, the more relaxed she became about the horns on her head. They no longer posed a hazard to her. Some of the older zebus showed her some tricks about how to position her feet so that she always had a strong center of balance. And nobody ever again made fun of her size. Every one of the herd knew that Zoe was the master gatherer of the tastiest treats, and being nice to her would mean delivery of at least one bunch of the greenest and most lush grass on the savannah.

Recognize what you can and cannot change. Don't waste time and energy on the 'cannot'. When you cannot change your situation then learn how to make the most of it.